Edward Richard  Shaw

**Legends of Fire Island Beach and the south side**

Edward Richard  Shaw

**Legends of Fire Island Beach and the south side**

ISBN/EAN: 9783743349834

Manufactured in Europe, USA, Canada, Australia, Japa

Cover: Foto ©Andreas Hilbeck / pixelio.de

Manufactured and distributed by brebook publishing software (www.brebook.com)

Edward Richard Shaw

**Legends of Fire Island Beach and the south side**

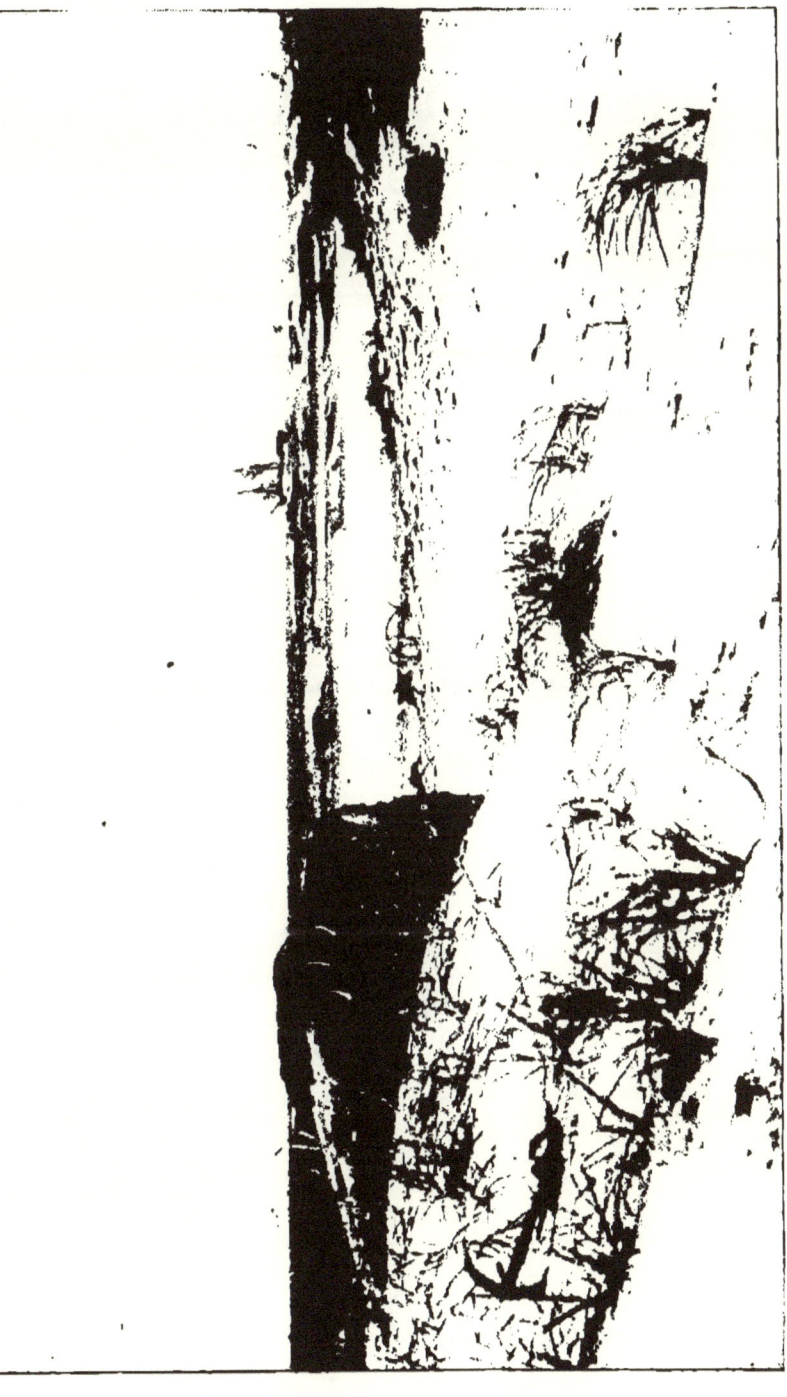

"A BARRIER OF SAND STRETCHING FOR TWENTY MILES ALONG THE SOUTH COAST OF LONG ISLAND"

# LEGENDS OF FIRE ISLAND BEACH AND THE SOUTH SIDE

BY

## EDWARD RICHARD SHAW

NEW YORK
LOVELL, CORYELL & COMPANY
310–318 SIXTH AVENUE

# PREFACE.

THESE stories embody only a small part of the folk-lore and tradition that pertained to the Great South Bay. They were told by a class of men now gone. Fact, imagination, and superstition—each contributed its part. In the tavern, among groups of men collected on shore from wind-bound vessels, at gatherings around the cabin fire, and in those small craft that were constantly going from one part of the bay to another, not only these tales, but others, irrevocably lost, were elaborated and made current in days homely and toil-some yet invested with an atmosphere of romance.

Many of the illustrations in this volume are reproductions from photographs taken by Mr. R. Eickemeyer, Jr., medallist of the Royal Photographic Society, on his visits to Long Island. The artistic excellence of Mr. Eickemeyer's pictures is widely known, and the author, in appreciation of his interest and kindness, desires to make here grateful acknowledgment.

BELLPORT, LONG ISLAND,
June 25, 1895.

# CONTENTS

" On old Long Island's sea-girt shore,
Many an hour I've whiled away."

# THE POT OF GOLD

FIRE ISLAND Beach is a barrier of sand, stretching for twenty miles along the south coast of Long Island, and separating the Great South Bay from the Atlantic ocean.

To reach it, you must make a sail of from three to seven miles, and once upon it, you find it a wild, desolate, solitary spot, wind-searched and surf-pounded.

Its inner shore is covered with a growth of tide-wet sedge, with here and there a spot where dry meadow comes down to make a landing-place.

The outline of this inner shore is most irregular, curving and bending in and out and back upon itself, making coves and points and creeks and channels, and often pushing out in flats with not water enough on them at low tide to wet your ankles.

A third of the distance across the Beach, the meadow ends and sand begins. This slopes gradually up for another third of the distance, to the foot of the sand hills, which seem tumbled into their places by some mighty power, sometimes three tiers of them deep, sometimes two, and some-times only one.

These sand hills are the most striking features of the Beach. The biggest of them are not more than sixty feet high, yet so hard a feat is it to climb to the top, and so extended is the view below you— on one side the wide Bay, on the other, the ocean stretching its restless surface to the horizon—that you feel yourself upon an elevation tenfold as high.

Through these hills the wind makes a great galloping, whirling out deep bowl-shape hollows among them, and piling the shifting sand upon their summits. Now and then you will notice a hill with its shoulder knocked off by the wind, and a ton of sand gone no one can tell where. In every storm their contour changes, and yet their general formation is so similar at all times that the change is seldom thought of. A coarse spear-like grass finds a sparse growth upon them, and does what it can to hold the sand in place; but it has a hard time of it, as its blades buried to their tips or its naked roots often testify.

But there is one part of this Beach that is ever much the same. It is a broad, shelving strip of sand between the hills and the sea, where the tide rises and falls, pounding and grinding, year in and year out—the play-ground and the battle ground of the surf.

On a summer's day, I have seen this surf so low and quiet that one could launch a sharpie upon it, single-handed, and come ashore again without shipping a quart of water. At other times it is a terror to look at —a steady break of waves upon the outer bar, with row after row coming in, rearing and plunging as they strike the shore. In such a sea there is no launching yawl or surf-boat, and no coming ashore.

When the tide is on the right moon and the wind has blown a gale from the south-east, the strand is entirely submerged, and people upon the main shore three miles away can see the surf breaking over the Beach hills.

Such a riot of sea and wind strews the whole extent of beach with whatever has been lost or thrown overboard, or torn out of sunken ships. Many a man has made a good week's work in a single day by what he has found while walking along the Beach when the surf was down.

"The Captain" knew all this and had patrolled that Beach scores of times.

Ten years had passed since the first time which laid the habit of wandering along the surf-shore apparently in search of whatever the sea had cast up. Sometimes a spar, sometimes sheets of copper torn from a wreck and carried by a high surf far along the strand, sometimes a vessel's gilded name, at other times only scattered drift-wood were the rewards of these lonely walks.

People about the neighborhood where the Captain lived, knew that at one time or another he brought these relics from the Beach; yet no one supposed that the finding of them was related to his life in any other way than mere happen so. Anyone who went upon the Bay at all was likely to land at the Beach. Once there, it was a natural impulse to go across and walk along the ocean side; for, at that time, early in

the thirties, it was widely believed that the
sea had wealth, and often threw it up upon
the shore.   Never, however, was it in the
least surmised by the Captain's neighbors
that these solitary excursions had woven
themselves in as a part of the texture of
his life.

Had, though, these good neighbors been
quick to perceive they would have noticed
one characteristic of the Captain, sufficiently manifest at times—that he was
always in the best of spirits when a storm
was raging.   At such times he had been
heard to remark, " This is a wild day, my
friend, but just such days is needed."

And it was not till years afterward that
neighbor Rob'son actually understood the
import of a strange remark made to him
by the Captain one stormy night, when the
wind blew fiercely from the south-east, and
drove aslant the thin rain which the low
scudding black clouds let down.

Mr. Rob'son had been belated and was
hurrying to get home.   The Captain, meet-

ing him, called out in the most cheerful of
tones, "Hello, is that you, neighbor Rob'-
son?" and giving him time for merely a
bare "Yes," he continued, "This is a mon-
strous night. Do you hear the ocean
pound over on the Beach? There'll be tons
of sand shifted to-night—tons of it; more'n
all the men out on a gen'ral trainin' day
could shovel in a year. You're in a hurry,
I see, neighbor. I ain't. I'm in no haste to
get in-doors. A great night like this fits
me. Somehow it puts new spirit into
me."

Was it the storm that made the Captain's
heart so buoyant and his mind so cheerful?
or was it because such days and nights
made more certain the realization of that
secret hope which had possessed him for
years?

So secret was this hope that even his
wife surmised nothing of it; for, happily,
she was not one of those unfortunate
women who are endowed with satanic in-
tuition, and whose lives thereby are made

miserable until they have followed up and chased into clear daylight all the dusky suspicions that flit, perchance, into their minds.

But although a matter-of-fact wife, she had, it must be confessed, noticed more closely than her neighbors the effect a storm had upon her husband; and she had learned to put off until such a time those various little requests about the house, which appear in a man's eyes so great a matter to get about, and which he usually puts off and shirks with an unaccountable dread.   Every little change, therefore, she needed, of driving a nail here, putting a shelf there, or the mending perhaps of a churn-dasher, he cheerfully made at those times; and she would often remark to him, " It's astonishin' how much you'll get done on a stormy day, and the harder the storm the more you'll manage to get through with."

If, however, these odds and ends were not finished during the storm, they were

suffered to go over, as the Captain was
certain to leave home early the next morning; and to any neighbor who chanced to
inquire for him, the reply was made that
he had gone upon the Bay.

" Gone upon the Bay." That expression
was in those days a most convenient one
for a bay-man. The persistent following of
the Bay for a livelihood at the present
time causes each man to hold closely to
one kind of work. But then, there was no
telling when a man set out from home how
his day would be spent—he might go oys-
tering or gunning, he might cast his nets
or waste his time sailing in search of what
he deemed better luck. Varying conditions of wind and weather and tide offered,
one day, one thing, and the next day,
something else; and what use a bay·man
would make of his day grew out of these
conditions and his own ambition.

The Captain, however, on the morning
after a storm, paid no attention to what
these conditions offered till he had visited

the Beach and sought again the realization of his hope. He never failed to be on there early on such mornings, to see what the wind and the sea had done.

And so it turned out upon this very day. There had been a sudden and violent storm the previous night, and the Captain had crossed the Bay and was making one of his solitary patrols of the Beach.

Across his shoulder was thrown his gun, as this he always carried with him. And although he took no silver with him, as certain gunners were known to do, to substitute for lead should there occur any emergency bearing the suggestion of witchery about it, yet he felt, in some way which he did not care to examine, more comfortable with his gun in his hand. He knew well all those stories of witchcraft and mystery about the Beach which superstition and imagination had set afloat in various localities along the "South Side." How the witches would come at night and rattle the latch upon old Uncle Payne's gunning house, and how the owner fastened the latch with a shilling piece, crept in the window, and invariably loaded his gun with a silver sixpence to blaze away at these midnight revellers, should he hear the slightest indications of their freaks. And how gunners, taking the surest aim at the wild duck that flew to their decoys, had oftentimes been baffled in hitting them,

finding, in such instances, the shot roll out
of the barrel as the gun was lowered.  And
how many a gunner carried a lucky-bone
in his pocket as an amulet against such
sinister misfortune.

He had heard, too, of that sheltered spot
on the north-west side of Watch Hill, in-
closed by a clump of old bayberry bushes
and low cedars, where searchers for money
had occasionally gone with a mineral rod;
and who, whenever they began to probe
for treasure, were always frightened away
by a huge black snake that wriggled itself
up the stem of a bush, and stretched out at
full length along the top of the foliage,
darting its tongue and hissing as if guard-
ian of the enchanted spot.  And more
marvelous still, the tradition of a stone,
circular and flat, bearing upon its surface
·the image of a man's face, that had at
times been run upon, near the Point of
Woods, but which never could be found
when deliberate search was made for it.

While the Captain thought he put no

real credence in these stories, yet he felt more or less apprehensive when upon the Beach. A sense of mystic awe, which he could not explain always possessed him there, and notwithstanding his disbelief in witchcraft, he would sooner have abandoned his quests than forego the companionship of his gun.

All the morning long, that idea which had come to him with strange force ten years ago, and which had engendered the secretly cherished hope, was uppermost in his mind. So strongly did it dominate his thoughts when he was alone by the ocean that it had forced itself into words. Over and over again he stated it as he talked to himself, adding this time one tradition, the next time another. No one was near to hear it. The very utterance cheered him and fed his hope.

Becoming somewhat tired in his patrol, for he had already walked fully seven miles, he ascended one of the sand dunes to reconnoitre the Bay, and assure himself whether any boat was making towards this part of the Beach. He saw only two or three sails abreast of Patchogue, and these were bound westward. Feeling, therefore, that he could take the time, he threw himself down to rest.

The day was clear and bright, with a light breeze astir. The wide Bay was blue in the sunlight. Near the hither shore he saw a long file of wild ducks sweep a grace· ful curve and flutter down upon their feeding ground. On the farther shore stretched the stately woodland, its whole extent broken only by the meadows about the creeks, and the few patches of green that revealed the scattered farms. This was all the prospect. No church spire stretched itself upward as a landmark, no village showed white along the shore, no fleet boats with pleasure-seekers sped here and there.

His weariness soon passed, and as he descended to resume his walk, the sand, flowing down the steep hillside as fast as he trod, set his thoughts back again upon the old theme. " The sand on this Beach is all the time a changin'. What are hollows now 'ill be hills in a few years. Sea and rain and wind are all the time at work. The wind, though, puts in the most time. How soon it 'ill sweep out a hole and carry the sand up the side of a hill anybody knows who has been on this Beach in a blow. It handles sand in about the same way it drifts snow.

" No, I'll never dig for treasure, and I've no belief in mineral rods. Too many fools have used 'em. Watch Hill has all been dug around ag'in and ag'in, and never anyone found a shillin' for all their potterin'.

If there's anythin' valu'ble buried on this Beach, sometime or other it 'ill be laid bare—that Money Ship wa'n't off and on here so many times fur nothin'—there's got to be treasure here, and who's more likely to find it than me? No man watches this Beach closer, and nobody knows I'm watchin' it, either. It'll come, too, one of these days! If a man's determined enough and only holds on long enough, what he's desirin' and hopin' for is sure to come round, else he wouldn't feel so sure about it all the time all through him. It'll come, it's sure to come, and then I'll build my vessel."

This had been the Captain's theory. He *had* held on. Never in the least had he slackened hope.

During the storm the tide had run high, surging up and washing away the foot of the sand hills. As far as his eye could reach, he saw the precipitous side of hill after hill. This very condition led him on a mile or more farther than he generally walked. And then, as no footprints but his own were to be seen anywhere on the crisp sand, he determined to go on still farther. He had walked perhaps half a mile, having lapsed into that state of reverie apt to come upon one who has urged himself beyond the accustomed limit of toil, when suddenly, through the drowsiness of his mind, a perception, unheeded at the time by the other senses, flitted back, awakening and concentrating all the faculties upon itself. In a moment he turned about, saying, "I believe I'll go back and see what that actually was that looked like a piece o' black glass midway up the bank." Reaching the spot, he stepped up the slope and began to dig away the sand. He saw at once that it was a small glass or earthenware pot of a blackish color, which settled quickly as he dug.

"Ah," exclaimed he, "the day's here! The day's got here at last!"

Clasping it in his hands, he weighed it, so to speak, lifting it up and down till his

surprised senses needed nothing more to
convince them.   He examined it, but found
no mark upon it, not even upon the resin
with which it was sealed.   Suddenly a
strange alarm rose up within him, and he
feared someone would come upon him. He
obeyed his first thought and looked quickly
eastward and then westward along the surf
shore, but saw no living form.   Someone,
though, might be crossing the Beach and
might at any moment appear on the crest
of the hill just above him.   Before the
thought which suggested this had really
passed, he began digging a place in
the sand, and in it he set the heavy pot.
The hole, however, was not deep enough,
and he lifted the pot out.   But thinking it
would take too long to dig the hole deeper,
he put the pot back again, took off his
coat, threw it over the spot, and laid his gun
atop of these.   With steps as agile as any
youth of twenty, he climbed up the slipping sand to the crest of the hill and
looked keenly over the Bay.   He found

himself as secure from interruption as when an hour or more ago he lay down to rest and enjoy the scene. In a second he had returned to the hole and was lifting out the pot, determined to open it at once.

Doubts, however, thrust themselves upon him. "Why had he taken so much for granted? What was really the need of all his alarm? After all the jar might only be filled with bullets or shot."

But another thought crowded closely along with these doubtful ones. "No, it couldn't be. He hadn't at last espied this jar—the only thing that met his hope for the countless times that he had walked along this shore—to find in it only lead. It had treasure in it of some kind. He was sure of it. His feelings told him so."

Opening his jack-knife he began to cut away the resin from the mouth of the jar, making slow progress with the hard covering. At length he reached the stopper, and tried to pry out the thick cork, but with such haste that his knife-blade broke,

and he was forced to cut down on one side
of the stopper. Deeming he had been a
long time opening the jar, his old alarm
returned, again suggesting that someone
might be approaching. A second time he
scanned the shore in both directions, covered the jar with his coat, ran up the steep
and looked over the Beach and over the
Bay. No sign of approach or molestation
was anywhere discernible. Condemning

the alarm that had so wrought upon him
in stronger terms than is necessary to use
here, he returned to the spot, and this

time, instead of kneeling, sat down and took the jar in his lap. Not a great while elapsed before he had cut away enough of the cork to thrust in the blunt edge of his knife. A pry, a deeper thrust, another pry, and out came the thick stopper. But now he was startled, fearing that he had opened some magical jar, and was, at last, to be entangled in that witchery he so strongly discredited ; for, strange to relate, upon looking in, he saw something that resembled either lint or cotton, and which no sooner had the air touched, than it slowly lost its substance and vanished. His affright went, however, as quickly as the mysterious exhalation, for there lay the coins of gold, as bright as on the day when Tom Knight, the buccaneer, afraid the town magistrate would search the Beach and find them evidence against him, had sealed the coins up in the jar, and hid it among the hills.

He tipped the jar aside to disturb the coins, observing as they slid over, other traces of the lint or cotton, which had evi-

dently been used to pack the coins in lay-
ers, either as security to the jar, or to
muffle any clink that would excite sus,
picion in removal.　But his purpose in tip,
ping the jar was not to witness the exhala
tion of the fluffy substance—he had an,
other object in view.　So, canting the jar
first towards him and then from him to se,
cure as varied a change of the contents as
possible, he peered to the very bottom.
Nothing there but gold, the yellowest of
gold.

Reaching in with two fingers, he brought
out a coin between them, and began to examine it.　The date, 1783, was all that was
familiar to him.　Looking at the other side,
he recognized the image of a crown, and
under it, upon a shield, figures of lions,
standing on their hind legs, with long tails
curved like the letter S.　Was it English
money?　The letters, HISPAN–ET–IND,
around the edge, were unintelligible to him.
He turned the coin back to the date side.
Here was the profile of some rotund person-

age, and over his head, CAROLUS III.
DEI–GRATIA. It was the *third* of some
monarch, that was evident enough; but the
DEI-GRATIA was just as puzzling as the
letters on the other side. Reaching in for
another coin, he read the date, 1799. Above
was a slightly different profile, the same
name, but after it was IIII. instead of III.
He drew coin after coin from the jar until he
had several in his hand. Except the dates
they were in the main alike. He conjectured
that they were doubloons—Spanish doubloons; and his conjecture was right. Sat-
isfied with the examination he had made,
he piled the doubloons in a column in one
hand, and with the other, lifted the pile and
let them drop, one by one, to hear the solid
chink. This, however, did not reach up
to the height of his feelings. So he spread
out his coat, and made, with a few blows
of his hand upon the yielding sand underneath, a concave surface. Then lifting the
pot, he poured out the coins in a glitter-
ing stream. Their fall was musical, and

when the last one fell, he scooped up double handfuls, held them high, and let the dazzling stream run again.

It was the first golden dream realized since the days when Captain Kidd was said to have buried his ill-gotten treasure in countless spots upon that Beach. How would that gold have dazzled the sight of all those argonauts who had made so many continuous but fruitless searches for the money reputed to be hid among those sand hills! What exultation would the sound of those falling yellow disks from the old mint of Mexico have wrought in those who had dredged persistently but in vain upon the bar where the long-boats of the Money-ship upset, or those who by moonlight and by starlight had walked to and fro over the hills, grasping the mineral rod, and digging where its delusive twitch indicated, until weary with toil and disappointment.

While the Captain's whole attention was completely absorbed in this revel with his gold, a coasting vessel had been approaching. It is true that the schooner was a mile or perhaps farther from the shore, "but with their spy-glass," thought the Captain, as he discovered the vessel, "those on board can plainly see just what I've got here." Hurriedly dipping up handful after handful, he slid the coins carefully into the jar, and after the stopper was replaced, wrapped his coat about it, reached his gun, and disappeared over the hills.

When he came to his boat, he tied the coat securely about the jar with odd strands of rope, and placed the prize carefully under forward. When night fell, it was his intention to make towards home.

The south-west breeze had gathered with the day, and blew freshly even from the Beach shore. Out in the Bay, where it had wide, unhindered scope, it had added to itself, pushing the waves before it, and urging them with such impetuosity that their crests grew flurried and broke into

white, foamy caps    Every leaf on the
" South Shore " was astir, fluttering and
tugging in the moist wind ; and the trees
bended and straightened to trim all their
spread of canvas to the sweeps of the
breeze.

"Ruther rougher than I care for to-
night," thought the Captain, "but the
wind'll fall after the sun sinks ; I'll give it
time."

The color had gone from the few strips
of cloud that lay about the sundown spot,
and the gray twilight arch stretched across
the west, as the Captain cleared away for
home.    Along the eastern sky, well up, a
glow of dull orange spread itself, and
creeping up to the glow and gradually
transmuting it, was a cold blue, the blue of
advancing night—a color so rare that it is
matched nowhere else than on polished
steel when the blacksmith tempers it.

The Captain steered with a strong and
steady hand, and watched his sail with a
vigilant eye.    But give heed as closely as

he might to his craft, there played with his
fancy the glowing rays of distant Fire
Island Light.   It had just been built.
Again and again its gleams, falling on the
dark side of some tumbling wave, caused

the Captain to turn his head and look over
his shoulder to the source whence they came.
The light was, in truth, no guide to him
on this night, but thoughts of the time
when it would be, kept recurring.   He
called to mind going in and out of Fire
Island Inlet years ago, before a light-house

was ever proposed, and of how difficult a
place the Inlet was to enter after nightfall.
But now, no matter how thick the night,
bring that light to bear north-east, and one
was inside and out of harm's way. What
an advantage it was! He thought, too, of
how he should see it far ahead, when
making a run homeward from Coney
Island; of the times he should have to lie
anchored within the inlet waiting for fit
weather to go out, and how companionable
that light would be sending out its bright
rays on wild, stormy nights.

All that the Captain fancied came true
in the years that immediately followed.
Speedily the timbers of a vessel were got
out and set up, and duly " The Turk " was
launched. What odd notion dictated the
name was never known. It was thought,
though, by many of his neighbors that some
name suggestive of that which made the
long-wished-for vessel a reality, should have
been given her. Indeed, there was no little
comment about it at the time, and much

protest whenever the vessel was discussed. It was overlooked, however, in this instance as it had been in several others, that the Captain held views and ideas quite opposite to those of most people who knew him; for what one of these neighbors, had he conceived the idea of finding buried treasure, would have done as the Captain did, and waited for the wind and the sea to dig it for him?

# THE BOGY OF THE BEACH

STRANGE things happen on that Beach and have happened. My experience was no new one, but it takes hold of a man, nevertheless, and he can't shake it off for months. Ever since white men frequented that Beach, some one at intervals has undergone the same foreboding experience.

In the early part of the last century a whaling crew, half Indians, had their hut east of Quanch. They used to land and come off at the point there, where the water is deep, called Whale House Point till this day. From the days of the earliest settlement, whaling crews used to go on the Beach. They would live there during the season and watch the sea day by day, ready to launch their boats and push off whenever they saw a whale blow. Their supplies were brought from the

north side of the Island, and fires were
built on Long Point as a signal for the
crew to come off.   The Long Point of those
days is now Ireland's Point, which pushes
out into the bay a mile, about, west of the
mouth of Carman's river.

When a fire flashed up at night, part of
the crew would row across the bay, heading
directly for the fire.   After they had put
the supplies in their boat and were ready ·
to return, they would throw sand on the
fire and put it out.   Soon after it disappeared a fire would blaze up on the Beach
to guide them back.   In that way Fire
Place got its old name.   That was a name
that had something behind it and never
ought to have been changed.

This crew had been expecting for three
days the signal fire.   They were getting
short of supplies.   People didn't get
around lively in those times, you know.
The trouble was that they hadn't much to
get around lively with.

For two nights until nearly midnight—

all this I heard from my great-grandfather
—the crew had set a watch on the top of
Quanch Hill to look out for the signal fire
upon Long Point. Now the curious thing
about this is that a man named Jonas was
the watch both nights. The first night was
his regular watch, but the second night he
volunteered to take the place of another
member of the crew. The men in the hut
spoke about this during the evening.
None of them, however, knew that Jonas's
idea was to satisfy himself as to whether the
strange experience he had had the night
before would repeat itself. That Beach,
you know, is one of the most lonely places in
the world. There are times when it's
awful on there. Take it on a dark night
with the wind wild and the sea mad.

That night Jonas made up his mind to
walk eastward a mile and a half. Frequently he would go down in the hollows
and stop to listen. He heard the sound
of the wind in the grass, and the beat of
the surf—each of these distinctly. And yet

something more. His heart began to
thump and his own breathing interfered
with his judgment. He tried hard to listen. Could he be deceived? he asked himself. Suddenly he turned and walked to the
top of a hill where no grass grew. He got
his breath and then held it. He heard even
the delicate beat of the particles of sand
blown by the wind, and he was sure that besides he recognized what he had heard in the
hollow. He could not be mistaken. Farther
away now, moving among the hills—almost
gone, then quite gone. The thought occurred to him then that he had forgotten
he was on the lookout. Immediately he
scanned the horizon to the northeast of
him but discerned no spot of flickering
red. He looked up at the stars to see
how far they had moved westward. Some
drifting clouds obscured two or three stars
he knew best, so he waited till the clouds
had shifted, and then he knew it was near
midnight. There was no use to watch
longer, for those who brought supplies

never made a fire after midnight. He turned to make his way toward the hut. He had not taken three steps, when he stopped and stood stock-still again. He heard distinctly the rumble and beat of the surf, the sifting of the sand, the sound of the wind in the dried beach grass, yet plainly apart from these something else. It moved on the wind rapidly away and away, and was gone. But as he stood thinking of it, it came again, stronger than before. This time not eastward of him, but clearly westward. His head grew hot. It moved farther and farther to the west, rising and falling, then with sudden increasing force stopped abruptly. He made his way to the hut and crept into his bunk. It was two hours before he got to sleep.

The next morning a whale was sighted close in shore. The crew launched their whale-boat and put off for him. They calculated where he would next rise and rowed to the spot. He came up lengthwise of the boat, just far enough ahead to smash it with his flukes. It was a right whale, and they strike sideways, you know, with their tail.

"Stern all," was the order quickly uttered. A short distance back, they whirled the boat around, and then pulled at the order. Whale-boats, I suppose you know, are sharp at both ends.

Before they were in position, however, to row straight on to the whale and keep clear of his flukes, he started. Quebax, the harpooneer, fastened his oar, grasped the harpoon, rose up in the bow and threw it. It was a long throw, fifteen feet, but it was the only chance. The harpoon entered the side of the whale and must have held securely. But the whale turned suddenly and struck the boat with his head. The crew sprang overboard just in time, for the next moment the whale stove the boat into flinders. The wind, so it happened, favored them, as it was blowing directly on shore. All the crew reached the Beach except Quebax. He was missing, nor was his body ever found. The bow of the boat, to which the line was fastened never came ashore, so it was thought that Quebax got entangled in the line. It was toward the end of the season—this whale would have made their sixth—and the disaster broke up their whaling for that year.

No man of that crew felt the great sense of relief at leaving the Beach that Jonas did, and never after would he go on there to remain overnight. He said nothing at the time about his weird experience among those Beach hills the night before Quebax was lost, but in later years he told it all.

And then, again, I have heard it said that for several nights before that awful catastrophe at Old Inlet, at the time of the War of 1812, the same strange calling and shouting was heard among the hills.

Old Uncle Payne, whose gunning house stood east of Molasses Island Point near Quanch, declared that twice in his life he heard at midnight the moaning in the hills, and each time thereafter had found bodies washed ashore.

But at Fiddleton, at Watch Hill, and through all the hollows there, down around Pickety Rough, even on Flat Beach, the eerie holloing, the shouting and calling, unlike any human voice, that was heard on different nights, suddenly changing, too, from one spot of the beach to another, foreboded the drowning of those fifteen buccaneers from the *Money Ship* and the burying in the sea for all time of their blood spent treasure. Yet having heard all this, though years before, I joined the first life-saving crew of Station No. —. The season then was a short one. Regular patrols of the Beach with exchange of checks for tally was then a thing undreamt of. Only in thick, foggy, or stormy weather did we walk the Beach. I can't see any use of patrolling that Beach in good weather and wearing the crew out. To my thinking all that is necessary on bright days or on clear starlight and moonlight nights is to keep a man on the lookout with a good glass beside him, and so save the crew; for there come times when the rescuing of life depends upon the reserve strength of the men. Yes, there come emergencies on that coast when power of endurance is the important, the decisive thing. The way to meet such unexpected demands and emergencies is to give the crew a chance to store up reserve force, power to hold on, to make a great effort for a night and a day, perhaps. This is what counts when a vessel is ashore far more than any regular patrolling, with the men on the go bright weather as well as bad weather.

We had pretty good weather that year till after the holidays had passed. Then there came a spell of thick weather. I remember distinctly how it set in. The day had been a very bright one, with a tinge of warmth in it. But at nightfall an ominous murky drift of cloud gathered in the southwest, a lee set for a northeaster.

The order was given for patrol that night, and the eastern beat fell to me. When the tide began to rise the wind hauled northeast by east and blew lightly down the coast.   It didn't seem to portend snow, but the weather began to thicken. I faced the wind and walked briskly, but it bit my face and searched under my clothing as only a northeast wind will do. When within a quarter of a mile of the end of my beat, I struck a match and held it between my two hands as a sort of a shield, and let it burn.   If you have never tried this, you have no idea how far such a light may be seen in the darkness or how large a spot of light it appears to make. Lanterns are of no account on that Beach. No lantern will burn when a high wind is blowing sand before it.   They choke up and go out.   And as about the only time when they would be of use is when they won't burn, they're not carried.   Then, after all, it's no place for them.   They'll do round the barnyard, but the coast is no place for a light, down almost on the surf's edge, bobbing and moving along in the darkness.

I lit another match and still another, but got no answer, so I concluded that the patrol up from the next station was returning. I reached the end of my beat, and waited some time under the lee of a hill, and near midnight began my patrol back. Passing a deep opening between the hills, my attention was attracted by a low moaning. At first I gave little heed to it. Then later I walked up to the top of one of the hills that flank the strand all along and listened. I faced the wind; then I stood back to it. I turned my ear in every direction, even bent my head down to render my hearing more acute. I could not distinguish any strange sound. No sooner, however, had I descended to the strand and resumed my walk than the moaning began again, seeming as before to be just over behind the hills. It was continuous but uneven, like the wind. It moved down the

Beach as I walked, just abreast of me apparently, but over behind the hills, considerably farther, however, toward the bayside when I passed any low spot of beach. When within half a mile of the station, it was gone. I noticed instantly when it ceased.

An experience of this kind disturbs a man's soul, and the more he fights it the greater trouble it becomes and the more uneasiness it gives him. But I said nothing about it at the station.

The thick weather continued. A seething, boiling surf was running, showing that there had been a big storm off shore. Such a surf always indicates that. We couldn't see much beyond the outer bar for several days.

In the next patrol at night I felt sure I should hear the moaning again, and I did. It followed abreast of me on my patrol out, and was gone as I approached the meeting-place at the end of my beat. But on my return it came again and followed in the same way as before. I didn't stop once to bother with it, but kept walking steadily back. It left me when about the same distance from the house as on the first night.

The next night my patrol began at midnight on the short beat to the west. I heard nothing out of the usual course of nature till I got within three-quarters of a mile of the half-way hut. Then I heard not only the moaning, but other noises not human, and a clapping or beating as with two flat sticks. All this was confined to one spot, and I could locate that spot exactly: in a rather deep hollow, with three hills butting up around. The wind from some cause always drew down into that hollow and kept its whole surface smooth, not a spear or root of grass there, and as round as the inside of a cup.

As I heard the voice, its hideous changes, which at times seemed to run into a part of some strange and weird tune, and the clapping along with it, I knew that all this foreboded some dreadful thing.

Hot flushes came over me and I sweat at every pore. But I kept on walking just as steadily as I could. I didn't want to quicken my pace a bit, and I had to hold myself down in order not to do it. I left the noises and clapping farther and farther behind, till at last I could not hear them. They didn't move, however, but remained right in that hollow. At length I came to the place where the half-way hut was, and turned up from the strand to go to it.

This hut stood well up in a sort of narrow pass that opened in a northwesterly direction through the surf hills. You could see the hut, coming from the east, but not from the west. It was built of old timbers and covered with seaweed and sand.

I entered, glad to get in there, and began to blow up a fire from the embers left by the patrolman from the west. I loaded my pipe and lit it, and the fire gave me some cheer. I stayed there an hour, I should think, dreading awfully to go. But

the thing had to be done, so I buttoned up my coat and started. As I came down to the strand suddenly I caught sight of something coming toward me dripping wet. The strength went out of my legs as quick as lightning, and my knees gave way. I nerved myself up at once, and there was need of it, too, for a voice—a human voice—called to me for help. It was a sailor who had just crawled up out of the surf. Instinctively I looked off shore and saw a vessel on the outer bar. She was not there an hour back, when I passed by.

The sailor sank down exhausted after he called to me. I helped him into the hut and blew up the fire.

" Are there any others ? " I asked.

" No," he replied, " I am the only one."

I laid on more fuel, left him, and walked along shore, looking into the surf with the keenest eye I had. I set off lights, but no answer. Then I went back to the hut, and the sailor had recovered sufficiently to give me a full account of how the vessel came on.

"We had thick weather for several days," he said, "and had lost our reckoning. We struck heavily on the bar off here, sounded, and made up our minds that we were on Nantucket Shoals, and that the only thing for us to do was to land. We hauled the boat up on the leeward side, the men got in, and I stood on the rail to cast off. Just as I had thrown down the painter, a big sea, coming round the stern of the vessel, struck the boat and turned her bottom side up. It happened in less than no time, for I had let go and had to jump. I struck on the bottom of the yawl and slid off into the sea. When I came up and put out my arms to swim, I struck an oar in front of me. This saved me. With it I worked toward the shore, but there I had a fearful struggle. Eleven times the waves threw me up on shore, but the undertow was so strong it carried me back each time. My strength was about all gone. The twelfth time a large wave carried me farther up. I felt the moving

sand under my feet, and, with the last rem-
nant of strength, I dug both hands and
feet into the sand with all my will, and
just kept myself from being carried back
again. I crawled up on the shore and
rested. When I got up to look around, I
saw a crack of light from the fire in this
hut, and I staggered toward it."

I summoned the rest of the crew, and
we had tough work the rest of that night
and for some days afterward.

But I was always apprehensive after this
experience and it weighed on my mind.
So in the spring I left the Beach, conclud-
ing that what I had heard and seen was
enough for one lifetime.

# THE MOWERS' PHANTOM

In the eighties of the last century, on
the sparsely settled old country road
north of Yaphank, two mowers were
arranging, one August evening, to go to the
Beach next day, and cut the sedge upon a
neighbor's meadow. "We must make an
'arly start," said Raner. "By sunrise we
ought 'o be well through the Gore in the
Hills. Arter wants that piece o' sedge all
laid to-morrer, ef we be men enough to do
it."

"How be you goin' 'cross?" asked
Layn.

"In the ol' hay-boat. I got her ready at
Squasux week ago yisterday. Josh Alibee
is to meet us there, so there'll be three on
us, you see. A big day's work, but we'll

take suthin' along to brace us up while we're doin' on it."

The sun next morning was not more than an hour high, when these mowers had embarked in the hay-boat for the Beach. The light breeze of that muggy August morning, blowing a trifle on the fore-quarter, carried them down the river so slowly that in order to gain time they plied the oar.

The scene which lay about them has changed but little in almost the hundred years which have passed since that morning. The river's course to the Bay was just as zig-zag then as it is now. Eastward lay the same broad meadows, skirted by that dense barrier of foliage—the Noccomack woods. Westward there stood upon the river bank where the Squasux road came down, a long, low one-story house, and below this the meadows extended to the distant woodland. As the sunlight fell aslant upon these meadows, they presented all those lustrous gradations of yellow and brown that may be seen in the early sunlight of an August morning to-day.

"There, put away yer oar, Josh; the breeze stiffens," said Raner, as they neared the mouth of the river.

"Thet ere's warm work," exclaimed Josh, as he finished the stroke and laid aside the oar. "I'll tek a swaller, I believe."

"No, no," replied Layn; "put that jug back. It's too 'arly in the day to begin swiggin' at that. You'll hev need o' ev'ry drop o' your share on the Beach."

"A couple o' swallers 'ill mek no dif-f'rence one way nur t'other. Not a sol'try horn hev I hed yet to-day, an' I've pulled the hull way down the river, whilst you've sot thar, yer elbows on yer knees," replied Josh, as he tipped the jug and drank.

"Pass it along," said Raner. "Our ends hev all got to be kep' even to-day."

Raner and Layn each drank, though lightly, and passed the jug back to Josh.

who, remarking, " It took all t'other swaller to wet my throat," deliberately tipped the jug and drank continuously as he walked forward to put it in its place.

The hay-boat went slowly, and the time passed tediously to men who were ambitious to be at their day's work.  Of this Raner himself furnished the best evidence, as he stood by the tiller, treading from side to side, and knocking one foot against the other.

The present generation has little notion of what the sailing of those days was, particularly in the flat-bottomed, square-ended hay-boats.  With a free wind, the course could be pretty well kept, but with the wind abeam, leeway became almost equal to headway, and wide calculations and allowances had always to be made.  Layn had this in mind when he said, " Give the Inlet a wide berth or I'm afeard the tide ll ketch us an' draw us through."

"She'll clear it, an' a plenty to spare," replied Raner.

"You better not be too sure 'bout that. I, for one, don't want 'o fare ez them Swan Crick fellers did."

"What Swan Crick fellers?" enquired Raner.

"Why, Mott an' a nother young feller— I dun know what his name wuz. Hain't you heer'd 'bout 'em?"

"No."

"Well, I hed 'em on my mind when I said, 'Give the Inlet plenty o' room.' You ain't heer'd on it, then? Well, this ere young Mott and t'other feller started out the Crick to sail their hay-boat somewheres east o' the Inlet. Ol' man Mott hed built the boat, an' hed put cleats on the edges under 'er sides, to keep 'er from slidin off to leward. She sailed smart, an' hung on to the wind purty good, I b'lieve. The ol' man, though, tol' 'em to look out fur the Inlet, an' give it a rattlin' good distunce. But, by George, 'fore they knowed it, they wuz goin' toward the Inlet. They tried might an' main, puttin' out poles an' doin' ev'ry thing they could, to steer 'er to shore, but no use. They couldn't reach bottom, fur she kep' right squar' inter the middle o' the channel, an' out she went.

"The poor devils wuz wild. The wind, what thar wuz on it, wuz blowin' from the nuthard. They lowered sail, but out to sea they kep' on goin'. Finely, arter they got out sev'ral mile, the wind changed to the suthard. They histed sail, pinted 'er straight on, an' beached 'er on the surf-shore off abreas' o' Muriches, an' the ol' man went down thar an' wracked the very boat he'd jist built,"

Josh, who had sat with his gun across his knees during Layn's account of this mishap, now resumed the work of cleaning his gun, upon which he had put all his time since clearing the mouth of the river. Priming the musket, he raised it to his shoulder, took an imaginary aim, and remarked: "She's in royal trim now fur any bunch o' snipe thet shows up on the medder"

"Where did you come upon that buster of a fire-arm?" inquired Layn, in jest.

"Thet ere fire-arm, le' me tell you, hez been proved. She's seen sarvice, but thet wuz afore I got 'er."

"Hain't she seen sarvice sence you've had 'er, ur plaguey nigh it?" continued Layn.

"Seen sa—ar—vice sence—I've — hed 'er?"

"Yes, by George, yes."

"You're talkin' to me in riddles."

"Why, Joshua," broke in Raner, "hain't there been orchards girdled, a barn burnt, an' thirty horses made way with by some on you Punksholers not a great while back?"

"Exac'ly," said Layn. "That ere hints the matter, Josh. Wuz that ere gun one on 'em that wuz drawn on Judge Smith, an' would a' done the mischief on 'im, hedn't his wife happened to keep atween him an' the winder whilst he wuz ondressin' a-goin' to bed?"

"Thar wuzn't but three on 'em at thet ere bus'ness, an' is it your idee to hint thet I wuz one on em? Ef it be, thet's hittin' devlish nigh—*devlish nigh;* an' I'm blasted ef I don't tek thet up," replied Alibee, spitting in his hands and stepping up to Layn.

"Nay, Joshua, nay; couldn't that flint-lock a been there without you, or at any rate, afore you owned it?" spoke Raner, to pacify Alibee.

Layn discerned that he had gone too far in his attempt at accusation, and so in a bantering way, continued, "You said yer musket had seen sarvice. You wan't in the Rev'lution'ry War, nur even in a skirmish. The wicked thing some o' you Punksholers meant to do on Judge Smith is known to the hull Town, an' you wuz a braggin' 'bout the sarvice yer gun hed seen. What harm wuz thar, by George, in askin' you, straight out an' out, ef that wuz the sarvice she hed seen?"

"A devlish lot o' harm, when a man

wa'n't thar, nur nowheres near thar, nur never hed an idee o' bein' thar," replied Josh.

"Trim in the sail now, an' quit your sq'abblin'," spoke out Raner. "There, that'll do. Now she p'ints up better, an' ef she don't slide off over much, we'll make our landin' spot without a tack. Ah! that's a strong puff."

Raner looked to windward thoughtfully a few minutes, and then began to whistle. The breeze, the onward motion of the boat, and the movement of the waves stirred his feelings, and he whistled on for a full half-hour.

As the craft approached the Beach, there came into view spots of meadow

"Where merry mowers, hale and strong,
   Swept scythe on scythe their swaths along
   The low green prairies of the sea."

These scattered groups had been upon the meadows all night, ready to begin at sunrise the toil of the day. And toil it was too—toil that required an iron muscle and iron endurance. Yet, toil and moil though it were, beach-haying was always a welcomed season. It broke the monotony of farm life. There was the sail to and fro, the breeze from the sea in its first freshness, the beat of the surf, the wide view on every side, the visit to the ocean at night, and often a race with the slow-creeping tide to determine whether the mowers should lay their stint, or the water usurp their place.

The three mowers had made an early start and were in good season, but the sight of others at work roused their anticipations of the day's labor, and Layn suggested, " Let's give our scythes a thorer goin' over. We'll save time by it."

They did this, and then Josh said to Raner, " Shell I put an edge on *yer* scythe ?"

" No," was the reply. " I'll do that fur myself. You come aft an' take the tiller."

Over the ocean, low down on the horizon, lay a bank of fog. The mowers noticed this, and Raner remarked, " It may

lay there all day, or it may clear away an'
be gone when the sun gits higher and the
day warmer."

" Thar's no tellin' nuthin' 'bout what
it'll do, you'd better say," replied Josh,
with a laugh.

All along they had feared the wind
would fail them when well over under the
Beach. But it continued to blow; and in
as good season as the mowers had hoped,
they reached the meadows. Josh stood
forward, anchor in hand, and jumping
ashore, walked the full length of the cable
and planted the anchor deep in the soft
meadow soil. The old sail was quickly
furled, and the three mowers, with scythes
and traps, set out for Arter's lot. Raner
led the way, carrying, besides his scythe, a
rake and hammer and wedges to hang
anew the scythes, if need were. Layn was
almost abreast of him, managing with some
difficulty his scythe, a pitchfork, and a run-
let of water; while Josh followed a short
distance behind with the jug. Watching

his chance, he lifted the jug and stole a draught.

"Le' me see," said Raner, approaching the place of their day's work. "Accordin' to the last division, the stake o' every lot stands on the west side, an' the numberin's on the east side o' the stake."

A little examination showed which Arter's lot was, and then Raner said, "We'll strike in here."

This was not the order to begin cutting, but for those immediate preparations which can be made nowhere else than on the exact spot. And so there followed driving of heel-wedges, twisting and ranging of blade with handle, stretching out of the foot to determine whether the scythe-point was too far out or too close in, and last, a stroke in the grass for final approval.

"We're all ready, then, be we?" asked Raner. "Well, I'll lead. Josh, you come arter me; an' Layn 'll be last;" and getting into position, the lusty mowers struck their swaths. Regularly the graceful strokes fell, succeeded by the hitching step forward.

"Ah! my scythe's doin' purty work, I tell you," remarked Raner. " How does your'n cut, Layn?"

"Royally."

" An' your'n, Alibee?"

"Never better."

" We're all well under way, then, an' the grass's in fair condition. Can we lay it by night, think you, Layn?"

"I guess so ; but by King George, we've got 'o keep movin', le' me tell yer."

" Alibee, can you stan' it to keep 'er jog-gin' all day long at this gait ? "

" Thet's what I come fur, I b'lieve, to do a day's work with the rest on yer."

There had been some sort of an under-standing between Raner and Layn when driving to the landing, that Alibee, who was a loud boaster, should do such a day's work as he had seldom done.  It is easy, therefore, to see why Raner was so partic-ular about assigning him the middle place. Raner and Layn were both excellent scythes-men, and with one to lead and the other to drive, Alibee must keep their pace all day.

Alibee, be it said, was not an energetic man.  Some of his acquaintances called him a "blower."   Had he been hired to go to the Beach and take two men with him to cut a plot of grass, there would have been mowing done as a matter of course ; but the day, nevertheless, would have passed easily enough.  The bouts would have been short ones, with a spell of whetting at each end. There would have been halts here and there, while he looked to see how the grass lay ahead, and whether it was down much or tangled. And when such pretexts failed, Alibee would have found it encouraging to count just how many swaths had been cut, and calculate how many more remained to be done. At midday, too, a long nooning would have been taken, with likely a stroll to kill a

mess of snipe. Let, however, a few months pass, and beach-haying become the topic of talk at a tavern gathering, and with what noisy bragging would Alibee recount what he and two others accomplished in two days last summer.

"There's the first bout round," remarked Raner, "an' now whet up fur the next."

"An' wet up, too," broke in Josh.

"Yes, yes," seconded Layn; "a good horn all round."

All drank; but Josh was last at the jug, and improved his opportunity.

Each man took up his scythe again, wiped the blade with a wisp of grass, and struck with drawing motion his rifle along the blade. Every blow sent out those ringing notes—the test of good steel.

The whetting over, *zithe—zithe—zithe—* went the scythes once more, the graceful strokes beating again their triple measure. But before the mowers had finished their second bout, the outposts of the fog, which lay banked low over the ocean when they were crossing the Bay, came and settled about them. So intent, though, were the mowers upon the work in hand, that the fog's insidious presence was not noted, till making the last stroke out, they straightened up and looked around. They could not at first realize the change. When they had struck in at the other end of the swath, their view extended over miles—the wide Bay and the blue shore beyond, lay to the northward; west and east stretched the meadows with their sinuous edges; to the south were the Beach hills and the gap through them, affording a glimpse of the ocean. What wonder is it, then, that the mowers, bending down and watching intently to see where the next stroke should fall, lost consciousness of their surroundings, and were, the first instant on looking up, bewildered to see the impenetrable gray on all sides?

"Well, I sw'ar," spoke Josh. "This ere's sudden—I'll be darned ef I knowed where I wuz for a second ur two."

"Nuther did I," replied Layn. "At fust, I tried to git my bearin's, an' it bothered me, fur thar wuzn't no bearin's to be got. Then I come to my senses, an' knowed I wuz right here on the medder mowin', with this ere bank o' fog all round us."

A fog, as everybody knows, plays all sorts of tricks with the judgment. A man may drive over a road a hundred times and think himself acquainted with every turn and hollow, with every clump of trees, with every bank, rock, or bunch of shrubbery by the roadside; but let a dense fog come down, and memory at once refuses to match the new impressions with the old. The hollows are deeper and the bends of the road more abrupt, the clump of trees has shifted its position or has entirely disappeared, and every rock and bunch of shrubbery becomes a strange object. If he begins to doubt, his judgment is completely upset, and he concludes he has taken the wrong road.

A man may have sailed from shore to shore of a body of water so often as to feel almost confident of doing it with eyes shut; let, however, a fog settle and blot out every surrounding object, and ten to one he will conclude, before he has sailed a mile, that he has not kept his course, or that the wind has shifted. Then it is all up with him; confusion and uncertainty follow, and there can be no telling where he will make land.

"What's it goin' to do, Raner?—hang here all day like this?" asked Layn.

"It acts to me, with this light wind a blowin', as ef there'd be lots o' fog adriftin' all day. But fog or no fog," replied Raner, "we mus' keep a steppin'."

At Raner's suggestion the stroke was

resumed, and the mowers gave no furthei heed to the fog whose mysterious depths had shut them in, and severed, as it seemed, all connection with the little world they knew.

Round and round they mowed, bout after bout, swinging their blades with the same lively stroke. For three hours Alibee stood the driving well, and then all of a sudden he broke out with, "This 'ere ain't squar'—it's urgin' the thing a little too much. My scythe's losin' her edge; the ol' rule is to whet at ev'ry corner, an' drink at ev'ry round."

"Well, ain't we drunk at ev'ry round?" answered Layn; "an' I took notice thet you swilled ez long ez any on us."

"Thet I'll 'low," said Josh; "but we ain't whet at ev'ry corner. Thet's my p'int. Th' ain't nuthin' much made, ez I kin see, by drivin' so like the devil. You'll wear me threadbare afore sundown, keepin' me here in the middle. It's the hardest place to mow in, by a darn sight."

" Joshua," said Raner, " I thought you Manor men wuz all such cracked mowyers. Here's Layn an' me, we're only common mowyers, an' you can't keep your end up with us, hey?"

"Yes, I kin," replied Josh; "but what's the use o' killin' yerself. We can't cut this ere medder to-day nohow, an' I don't see the use o' workin' hard ez you kin swing, an' goin' home middle to-morrer to do nuthin' all the arternoon. By gosh," he continued, sighing, as if partly exhausted, " I'm darned ef I don't b'lieve some sort o' contrivance could be rigged up to do this ere mowin'."

"What sort o' a contrivance, Josh?" quickly inquired Layn.

"Why, thar could be three ur four scythes hitched on to a post to swing round, an' cut twice ez fast ez we're doin' on it. An' one o' these ere days some ere feller'll rig up jist sich a machine."

"Not in our day, Joshua," laughed Raner.

" No, no; not in our day," repeated Layn, joining in the laugh.

" Your laughin' don't 'mek no dif'runce. I tell ye, I b'lieve it'll come yit."

" Why don't you try it yerself, ef yer so confident?" asked Layn.

" I'm bedarned ef I don't b'lieve I could, ef I hed time, an' tools, an' all the traps thet's wanted fur sich things. Them scythes, don't ye see, could be rigged to go roun' jist like thet;" and here Alibee cut a stroke to show what he meant. "Yes," he went on, growing earnest over his vague idea, "you could rig jist about three strappin' good scythes on to a post to swing roun' jist ez easy ez thet;" and here again he cut a dashing stroke.

" What a cussed foolish idee that is, Josh," spoke up Raner, a little vexed at the absurd notion. "How the devil, I'd like to know, would you make the post go?"

" Thet ere could be done somehow ur nuther. Thar'd be a way hit on, if a man taxed his noggin' long enough," replied Josh, hesitatingly.

Raner and Layn again both heartily laughed, and Josh said nothing more upon the subject. Whether, though, it was his remonstrance, or whether Raner thought they would thereby be able to cut more grass, he gave word at the next corner to stop and whet. This change put Josh in better spirits, for when the whetting was finished, he remarked, "Thar's only jist one thing a lackin', and thet's the jug. Ef thet ere jug could only foller us roun', we couldn't ask no more."

"Ef it did," said Layn," you'd be all the time a guzzlin'."

" I ain't no bigger guzzler than you be," retorted Josh.

The morning wore on, and it seemed to Alibee that noon would never come. Every stroke went against his will. At one time he was on the point of deserting, and leaving Raner and Layn there to drive each other; but seeing how dense the fog was,

and remembering he had no other way
of getting off the Beach than to walk three
or four miles east to the groups of mowers
they had passed in the morning, and fearing that he might get lost should he attempt this—a thought which made him
shudder—he held himself in control. The
fog at this time was so thick that one could
not distinguish an object four rods away,
and the impossibility of measuring with the
eye what had been cut, and what yet remained of the plot apportioned for the
morning, was disheartening to Alibee. To
his mind it seemed an endless cutting in a
prison of fog. If, however, he had lost cal-
culation and had thereby become dispirited,
the plot was lessening just as rapidly as if
in full view from start to finish. And
shortly after midday, the mowers walked
up the last narrow strip, leaving the morning's stint all laid.

" Now fur a chance at what victuals we
fetched along. You go to the hay-boat,
Josh, arter our pails, while Layn an' me

heap up some o' this grass to set on whilst we're eatin'."

"Gi' me a swaller fust," replied Alibee; and after satisfying his thirst, he started for the hay-boat.

Ten minutes passed, and out of the fog came a voice, "Which way be yer? How fur be I frum the boat?"

"This way o' you, an' to the nuthard," replied Raner. "Don't you hear the surf to suthard o' you?"

Groping about a little longer, he found the boat and soon came out of the fog with the dinner pails.

The mowers, to state it as they would, lost no time in falling to. Their fare was plain—plainer, indeed, than was usual at home. But though plain, the labor near the sea had whet their appetites, and they ate with keener relish than at their own tables. Then, too, the jug came in and played its part rather more freely than it would have done at home. They talked of the morning's work, and discussed the probabilities of cutting the rest of the meadow that afternoon and getting away for home before sundown.

"We ain't laid but little more'n a third on it," remarked Layn.   "It's my opinion we'll hev to stay here on the Beach all night, an' cut the balance 'arly to-morrer mornin'.   Then, ef thar's any wind, we kin reach Squasux landin' middle fore-noon."

"Thet's the idee exac'ly," replied Josh. "Tek it easy this arternoon, quit work arly, an' I'll hev a chance to git a bunch o' snipe.   We kin git home at noon to-morrer at thet rate, jist ez easy ez you kin toss up yer hat."

"What 'o you say 'bout it, Raner?" asked Layn.

"Well, I wanted to git off to-night, but ef we're goin' to do it, we've got to cut faster this arternoon then we hev this mornin'," replied Raner.

A half hour was all the time taken for dinner.   Layn carried the pails back to the boat, and the mowers finished their rest by whetting their scythes carefully, giving them a keener edge than they would take time for in the midst of work.

" Ef we're all ready fur work ag'in," said Raner, " we'll cut in this d'rection this arternoon. Down here an' up ag'in on the west side o' the lot, ef we kin see where the west side o' the lot is."

Alibee fell into his old place without a word of complaint. Raner began with the stroke he had maintained all day, but it was evident that Alibee intended to make his stroke in slower time, while Layn was not so anxious to drive him as he had been throughout the morning.

An hour passed, and Raner, after pacing over what yet remained uncut, remarked, " We can't poke along in this way, ef we've got any idee o' layin' this piece afore night. We come on here to cut, an' fur my part, I want to git done and hev it over with."

" This 'ere's good 'nough," replied Josh. " Let it go et this."

The wind, they noticed, was blowing stronger, and the fog began to sweep past them in dense scuds, at times suddenly growing thin as if about to clear away. Occasionally a yellowish tinge overhead gave indications that the sun had almost broken through, but presently a thick scud would come and shut the mowers in again. Thus, with fantastic behavior, the fog came and went. Two or three times, when it came the thickest, and darkened rapidly about them, they broke their stroke and looked around.

"Fust it's dark an' close, then it's lighter, then it'll come in agin thick, an' then, the nex' thing, the sun all but breaks through it. What a witchin' sort o' an arternoon it is," said Layn.

"I'd a darned sight ruther it ud gether itself up an' shower. Then thar'd be some likelihood o' the sun's comin' out an' dryin' on it up," replied Josh. "This ere thick an' thin, dark an' light, I don't like. Raner," he continued, "you couldn't a picked a wuss day."

"I never knowed sech a day afore in my life," spoke Layn. "Miles o' this fog has been runnin' by us all day long, an' this arternoon it's a loomin' itself up an' meltin' away ag'in in all kinds o' shapes."

The long swaths they were now mowing lay in direction to and from the ocean, and the place where the bouts ended and the indispensable jug stood in readiness, chanced to be so situated with reference to the gap between the hills that it afforded a view directly out upon the sea. The nature of the fog made this view more or less indistinct, at times shutting it entirely out of sight. Here the wind would bank up the fog, twist it into fantastic shapes, and blow them all away, only to summon more of the pliant medium and heap it up again into more grotesque masses. The mowers, dull as their perception was, at last saw this, and it wrought upon their minds. The feeling kept coming up that the appearances which the fog assumed through the gap were due to some kind of witchcraft.  All the superstitious stories they had ever heard about the Beach vividly recurred to them, and these idle tales now assumed the very force of truth; and so they approached each time the spot that opened up the view, with increasing dread.  They slighted their whetting at this corner, and would not have stopped at all had the jug been elsewhere.  Alibee's apprehensions that what he had seen through the gap boded evil to them, were the first to get the upper hand of him, and suddenly stepping ahead and cutting the first stroke, he broke out, " By thunder, gi' me a chance to lead *once*.  I'm darned ef I'm going to stay on this ere Beach to-night, nohow."

Raner and Layn were startled by this sudden freak of Alibee's, but they fell into line and followed with quicker stroke than they had heretofore made.  Alibee proved himself equal to the place he had assumed, and the next corner was quickly reached. Here the whetting was done with new energy, and the scythes flew again.

" Keep 'er up, Josh," urged Layn; " we're hard on ter you. I ain't got a bit more notion then you hev o' stayin' on here all night."

They came round again to the dreaded corner. Alibee grated his teeth as he thought of it, and his breathing was hard enough to be heard by the others. Coming out first and looking seaward, the very thought he intended not to mention slipped from his control, and he spoke out, " Thar she is ag'in." But recovering himself to some extent, he turned quickly about and continued, " Layn, you lead this time. Then it'll fall ekal on all on us. Ev'ry man's got a dif'runt stroke, an' ef he leads once, mows in the middle once, an' follers once, he gits a chance one time ev'ry three, to swing his nat'rul stroke."

Stepping to the jug he took it up and, shaking it, resumed, " I swar, we ain't got

but 'bout one good horn apiece, and thet
puts us in a hell-sight wuss fix then we're
in now."

They drained the jug to the last drop,
and bent again to their work. The pace
they were keeping was exhausting, but
they never slackened. Another bout was
finished within a dozen strokes, when
Layn burst out, " Here we come ag'in to
thet blasted gap. My blamed eyes won't
keep away from it whenever we git roun'
here."

"*You've* seen it, then, hev yer?" asked
Josh.

" Hang it, yes," replied Layn; "an' I've
tried *not* to, fur three times now."

"So hev I, an' I seem hell-bent to look
thet way whenever I git roun'."

Raner said not a word. It was his turn
to lead, and he started in without suffering
the talk to go further. They were working to the utmost of their strength. Layn
and Alibee cut wider swaths than at any
previous time. They reached the end, and

Layn said, "Raner, you go to t'other end, an' roun' thet corner, so we kin mow by thar without stoppin'. Josh an' me'll cut across this ere end, so's not to lose no time."

Raner complied; but the others noticed that instead of returning the instant he had accomplished the purpose, he stood a moment and looked out through the gap.

When he returned, Layn could not refrain from asking, "Did you see it?"

"Yes," replied Raner, "an' I swar I don't like it."

They plunged into work again with greater determination. It was in this way they kept their courage up; for every time they stopped to whet, their feelings were in a turmoil. The very pace they were working put them in all the worse condition. But the plot was lessening rapidly, and so they drove themselves on. Strange to say, some time passed without a word further in allusion to what had been seen. But while there was for this short period a dogged spell upon them to say nothing

more about what each was sure the other
had seen, the very bugaboo in their minds
made all the more headway because of their
silence; and in spite of themselves, they
kept glancing through the gap, when they
cut across the end where the empty jug
lay. The expedient of curving that end
did not dispel their alarm, for when they
rounded the broad curve, some sinister influence impelled them to look seaward.

"She's fog color," abruptly exclaimed
Josh, startling both Layn and Raner, and
causing them to look at the same instant.
"She's got ev'ry stitch spread, too."

"An' still headin' right squar' on, I
sw'ar," said Layn. And pointing, he continued, "Raner, do you see? We ain't got
no sich breeze a blowin' here ez she's got
thar."

"What the hell's dif'runce, tell me, does
that make with *her?* That wizard o' a
ship 'ud have fair wind an' plenty on it, ef
she wuz sailin' dead to wind'ard."

"Now, she's gone ag'in," spoke Alibee,
"an' thet's what she's done afore."

The mowers began a new bout, and Raner remarked, " Such things, hell take 'em, have been seen afore, though a long time back. I heerd tell on 'em when I wuz a boy. It's a spectre o' some ship Kidd has sunk with all her crew on board, a ha'ntin' this coast. Thar's no tellin' what the mischief'll come out on it all to us, ne'ther. He wuz off the Inlet thar sev'ral times with the ' Royal Eduth.' I've hearn, time and ag'in, o' how he come in the Inlet with his long-boat, an' got game o' the Injuns, an' the devil may know how many lives he put an end to when off here."

The mowers came again to the bout leading up to the broad curve. Alibee, who a moment ago had said, " I'm all o' a cold sweat," looked out upon the ocean and exclaimed, " By the very devil himself, see how much nigher she's in ! Confound ef I want 'o stay here an' cut much longer."

This exclamation produced but one result—a wider swath. They had plunged into deeper stroke that afternoon after every expression of fear, for the mowers tried, in the prodigious effort put forth, to drown, for the moment, their apprehensions. But the drafts they had made upon their strength were now telling upon them sorely. They could not sustain the effort, and soon lapsed into a slower stroke; and although the bout was considerably shorter, they were a third longer in cutting it. Though wrought to the highest point with fear, they were powerless to resist the bewitching influence to look seaward as they mowed round the curve. This time that strange shape, looming up again, struck terror through them.

" By heavens," gasped Alibee, " how much closer in is she a comin' ? An' look! look! thet's a woman standin' on the rail thar, for'ard, white ez the ship. Not another soul on board, ez I kin see."

The mowers stood gazing a second with scythes poised, and then finished their strokes. Just around the curve Alibee stole a glance behind him. With piercing tone he cried, "Good God! thar's thet

woman, on the hills yunder, comin straight
fur us; an' the ship, look! she's bow on.
Quick, quick, run fur the hay-boat."

Hurriedly they gathered their traps and
ran to the boat, casting looks behind every
few steps. They had left the jug—the
empty jug—but not a second could be lost.
They threw their scythes into the boat,
Alibee ran for the anchor, and came running back with it, dragging the cable after
him. Raner and Layn in their excitement
had already pushed off the boat, and Josh,
splashing through the water, tumbled on
board, anchor in hand. In an instant the
mowers had disappeared in the fog.

# ENCHANTED TREASURE

Purty nigh a hull week that ship hed
been seen manoovrin' outside the Beach.
Fust, she'd 'pear to be purty well in, an'
then she'd be way off a'most out o' sight;
an' so it went, off an' on, off an' on. The
neighbors—thar wa'n't many on 'em, the
houses bein' scatterin'—hed seen 'er; an'
thar wuz a good deal o' conjectur 'bout
what she could be doin'. Nobody
could tell. Thar wusn't no war—ef that
hed 'a been, 'twouldn't 'a been 'tall puz-
zlin' what she wur a-manoovrin' at on the
coast. On a Friday arternoon she dis'-
peared, an' nothin' wuz seen o' her on a

Saturday. Sunday mornin' 'arly, I looked over to the Beach, but didn't see anythin' o' the ship. She'd gone fur good, we concluded.

Long middle forenoon, John an' me made up our minds to go to the Beach. It wuz hossfootin time, an' that night wuz full moon. We put up suthin' to eat, an' told the folks to hum that we wuz goin', an' didn't calc'late to be back till long towards nex' mornin'.

Our plan wuz to sail over, saunter long the Beach that arternoon, an' 'bout nightfall git a pen ready to put the hossfeet in, an' when the moon wuz up an' the tide flood, ketch all the hossfeet we could. That's the best time o' the month to ketch 'em—full moon and flood tide.  Hossfeet, you know, crawl up in pairs on to the shore at the height o' the flood.  You wade along an' find 'em in the edge o' the water; throw 'em up onto shore high and dry, an' stick their tails into ground.  They're fast, then.  You got to work quick, 'cause the nick o' the tide don't stay on long.  It's git all you kin afore they go off.  When they're gone, you kin take your own time in loadin' 'em into the boat, ur puttin' 'em into pen till you kin take 'em off.

John an' me intended to put 'em in a pen, let 'em be thar till we could bring on the scow to load 'em into, and then tow 'em off.  One year we got purty nigh three thousan' hossfeet in one night.  It's ex- citin' work to wade along, lookin' close to see em, fur the water's dark an' they're dark; ur else hittin' 'em with your feet, an' then reachin' to find 'em.  You got to be more'n car'ful, though, 'bout one thing, an' that's not to git their tails stuck into yer feet ur hands.  Ef you do, an' it goes in deep, ten chances to one you're a "goner."

Well, John an' me expected to mek a big haul that night. We went down to the landin, an' fussed 'roun' thar, gittin' the old skiff ready. We warn't in any hurry, fur we hed all day afore us. 'Twur one o' them shiny, quiet June days, an' it bein' Sunday made it 'pear all the more so.

The Bay wuz ez blue ez could be—the water wuz becomin warm—that's what made it blue. Thar wuz only a little mite o' wind, jist enough to fill the sail.

I remember that sailin' ez plain ez if it all happened yisterday. I steered part o' the way, then John took hold, an' I stretched myself out in the skiff. The sun shun warm—that kind o' pleasant warmth that you wanted to let soak in an' in.

The skiff slid for'ard easy—no tuggin' an' jumpin'; the waves—the water wuz only roughened a little—rippled an' slapped up alongside, soundin' holler to me in the bottom of the skiff, an' the water bubbled

aroun' the rudder—that's 'bout all thar
wuz to it, but somehow I could 'a sailed on
for a fortni't.

The tide wuz low when we got across,
but we had no diffikilty to git close to' the
medder, ez John steered up into a dreen.
We took out the mast, rolled the mutton-
leg sail round it, an' drawed the skiff up
into the grass. Then we eat somethin', put
the rest o' our victuals away till night, an'
went over to the surf shore. Thar we set

down a short spell, jist ez ev'rybody does,
I guess, when they go over to the ocean an'
have a plenty o' time to spar', ez we hed.
Fin'ly we begun our walk 'long shore to see
what we could find.

This ere walk 'long shore wuz one reason
why we'd come over to the Beach in the
forenoon. I don't remember how fur we
walked, but we sauntered along an hour or
so—the sun wuz quite a piece to the west—
when all on a sudden John p'inted off shore
an' says, " Jess, look-a-thar. What do you
mek o' that? Thar she is ag'in standin'
right onto shore."

" That's her," says I; " that's the same
ship, an' she ain't a-beatin' nuther, with the
wind this way." I somehow kind o' felt
that that ship wuzn't standin' close in fur
no good puppose, and I didn't care to be in
sight on-shore, ez thar hed been no end o'
strange things done on that Beach fust an'
last. I thought quick o' what, accordin' to
all accounts, hed happened in my gran-
ther's days, an' even thirty year back, in

my father's, so I says agin to John, " Come, let's git up in the hills out o' sight."

In less 'an no time, we slipped round the hills, climbed up one on 'em to where we could could jist peek over, an' laid down. The ship kep' a comin'.   She didn't seem to change her course by a yard's breadth. Ev'ry sail wuz spread an' pullin', an' I tell you she wur a purty sight to look at.

'Fore long, John says, " Jess, that vessel's got some puppose, an' we'd better go east."

So we scooted 'long behind the hills, an' ev'ry low gap atween the hills we come to, we'd stop car'ful an' look out to see ef the ship kep' on the same course.   Ev'ry time we looked out, she wuz nigher an' nigher. When we'd got a stretchin' good piece east we didn't run any further, but crawled up a low hill to take a good look-out agin. By this time, the ship wur pretty well in. Afore long, she rounded up into the wind, clewed up her squarsails, an' anchored.

"What're they doin' now, John?" I asked; "kin you mek out?"

"Lowerin' a yawl, it looks like to me," he says.

An' so they wuz. In a short time the yawl pushed out from the ship, an' then I could see plain enough what it wuz, an' that some on the ship's crew wuz comin' ashore in that ere yawl.

We hunted round fur a place to hide, 'cause we knowed they couldn't be a-comin' ashore fur water. There wuzn't no water to be got. Behind us wuz a clump o' cedars purty thick, so we run 'long a windin'

holler, an' crep' up into that bunch o' low
cedars. When we looked out, the yawl
wuz behind the hills; but purty soon it
come into range near shore, an' disappeared ag'in, fur the way on it wuz, thar wur
a small gap 'tween the hills that give us
this sight o' the yawl. Arter the yawl got
across that gap, we waited a long time—I
tell you it wuz long—afore we see anythin'
more on 'em. We got scared a-waitin'; fur
how could we tell but what they wuz
mekin' towards us? While I'd got sort o'
tired a-strainin' an' lookin' here an' thar,
an' fell to conject'rin' what under the sun
wuz goin' to turn out on it all, John says
all on a sudden, "Jess, look, thar's one on
'em on yunder hill."

I looked quick, and thar stood a sailor
with a spy-glass searchin' in ev'ry d'rection. We crouched flat, scratchin' our
hands an' face in gittin' under the branches
near ground. We'd a been layin' down all
the time, but a spy-glass is purty fur-
sighted, an' we knowed it, so we crawled

under the branches to be all the more out o' sight.

In jist about three minutes the sailor wuz gone. Then we hed another time o' fearin' what 'ud come next, but soon some men 'peared on the top o' the hill. Thar wuz five on 'em. I breathed hard, an' so did John, till we see they wurn't comin' towards us. They wuz carryin' somethin' *heavy*, ez they'd stop, set it down, an' take turns. An' when they changed what they wuz carryin', they changed shovels. They hed shovels with 'em, for these we could see plain enough.

These five men went onwards to a hill in the middle of the Beach—the highest hill within sev'ral miles—an' stopped on the side o' it toward the ocean. They stopped a long while an' 'peared to be takin' certain ranges. Fin'ly they begun to dig. Ev'ry single one o' the five wur a-diggin'. The bank o' course kep' a growin', and got so high, ur the hole got so deep, I dun know which, that we couldn't see 'em any longer

a-diggin'. Nex' they all come out, took
what they hed fetched with 'em, and put it
into the hole.    Then thar wuz a long halt
—all on 'em down in the hole.    Not one
on 'em wuz seen fur a long time.    That
time they wuz out o' sight so long that
John proposed to skulk to our boat.

But I says, " No, we wun't run  no risks."

He wuz afeard, an' so wuz I.   We hadn't
even our old flint-locks with us.  They
would a'boostered up our  courage consid-
'rable.    I wuz right, though, 'bout stayin'
where we wuz.   We shouldn't a hed  time
to get half way to our boat, 'fore they come
up out o' the hole, an' begun to shovel the
sand in agin.   I couldn't mek out but four
shov'lin', but  I never thought  much on it
at fust.   When the hole, though, got purty
nigh full—you could sort o' tell by the banks
—I couldn't then mek out  but four men.
I strained an' looked till there wuz dark
spots a-swimmin' 'fore my eyes, and then I
whispered to John—for  we  wuz  to  the

wind'ard on the men—sayin', "John, how many do you mek out a-shov'lin' ? '

"Four," says he, "only four, an' I been countin' 'em agin an' agin."

"That's all I kin mek out uther. Didn't five on 'em come ashore?"

"I know thar wuz five," says John; "I see them five jist ez plain ez I see them ere four now. I counted five on 'em in two dif'runt places."

The hole wuz filled, they spatted on the sand with their shovels—that ere made me all the time think o' buryin' somebody—an' then them four sailors went back to the yawl.

John an' me waited and watched another long, tejus time—I suppose they wuz a-waitin fur the best chance to git their yawl through the surf.   It's easier to come on, you know, than it is to git back agin.

Through that ere gap 'tween the hills, though, we see the yawl ez they rowed off to the ship, and we breathed consid'rable easier.   Anchor wuz huv up, the sails un-clewed, an' the ship tacked off to suth-'ard.

The days is long that time o' year, an' it wuz well onto sundown afore the ship got under way.   When we see she wuz headin' off, we made fur our skiff.

We gin up all idee o' hossfootin' that night.   It wuz too bad to leave the Beach, but we hed no mind to stay thar.   We wuz mighty afeard, you see, an' thar's no use o' denyin' it—the thoughts o' what be-come o' that fifth man wuz boogerish; so we put for hum.

It would 'a been one o' the very best nights for hossfootin'.   The tide wuz high, an' the moon come up over the Beach big an' full; but the Beach lay all dusky an'

dark under the moon, an' the night seemed
owly. We laid our course straight across.
It wurn't pleasant sailin', though, ez it hed
been in the mornin'; fur the waves kep'
mekin' moanin' noises an' guggling's all
'round the boat. I wuz chilly, an' my
feelin's crawled over me, and kep' crawlin'
over me till we got to the landin'.

The folks wuz su'prised to see us. We
got hum 'bout bed-time, an' told at once
what we'd seen; an' instid o' gittin' off to
bed 'arly, ez we al'ays did Sunday nights to
git a good start Monday mornin'—instid o'
gittin' off to bed, we all sot up an' talked a
long spell about it.

When I went to bed I couldnt' go to
sleep, 'cause I kep' thinkin' over the hull
matter. That day an' that ere bright
night hev al'ays seemed to me jist like two
days into one. Thar wurn't any daybreak,
fur the moonlight wuz ez bright ez daylight, an' you couldn't tell when one went
an' another come. I s'pose though, arter
all, that wuz a nat'rul thing in June, when

the sun rises 'arliest in the year; but I never noticed it afore ur sence.

Two ur three days arterward, some o' the neighbors stopped to the house in the edge o' the ev'nin', an' mongst other things that wuz talked over wuz that ere ship; fur, you see, she hed been noticed by all the people o' that section the week afore, an' now she wuz gone—nothin' more'd been seen o' her. I told what John an' me hed seen, an' so the story got afloat. All summer long, way into fall, neighbors an' people livin' quite a distance away would stop and ask me 'bout it—full a dozen men from the middle o' the Islan' stopped, fust an' last, to ask me if it twan't the same ship some o' their mowers see, one foggy day six weeks later on, when they wuz on the Beach cuttin' salt hay. Winter nights, we now an' then would git to talkin' it over 'round the fireplace. Well, time went on, an' young people ez they growed up would ask me to tell it to them.

I've told it a good many times—a good

many times. You see, it wur over fifty
year ago sence it happened.

"Did anybody go to the spot an' see
what wuz buried thar?"

Some dare-devils from away West somewheres tried to dig thar. They took a
clear night with only a little wind a-blowin'
an' a few clouds afloat, but when they got
fairly to work, it grew pitch dark, an' foggy,
ez quick ez a candle goes out. The air
got so thick they couldn't scarcely breathe,
an' then a skel'ton ghost with a dagger in
its hand, that hed some kind o' pale flame
creepin' an' burnin' on the blade, 'peared
right above 'em. It stood a minute an'
shook the dagger, an' then begun to move
'round 'em, comin' nearer an' nearer, till
the men run headlong fur their boat,
shakin' cold, they wuz so scared.

I heerd one on 'em say, ten year arter,
that that wuz the only time in all his life
his hair ever stood on end.

But nobody round here never dug thar.

They never even probed thar.  They never
tried the min'rul rod thar nuther, ez they
did sometimes in other spots.  Ev'rybody
roun' this ere part o' the Islan' knowed
better.  The treasure buried thar wuz enchanted treasure.  Nobody meddles with
enchanted treasure that knows what enchanted treasure is.

"What made it enchanted?"

That fifth man wuz a pris'ner they'd
taken frum some ship they'd run down,
robbed, an' destroyed with the rest on the
crew.  They'd got ready to come ashore
to bury treasure, an' they ordered him to
go long with 'em to help do it.  He went,
doin' his part o' the work jist ez ef he wur
one o' the gang.

They go ashore, mek up their minds
'bout the spot, take their ranges so they
kin come back to the spot when they want
to, an' then begin to dig.  When the hole
is dug deep enough, they set the treasure

into the hole, an' all stan' in thar aroun' it. The leader o' the gang tells the pris'ner that he's got to stay by that ere treasure an' guard it, so nobody kin ever git it but them.

They mek him sw'ar with some kind o' an oath that he will. Then they mek way with him, an' put his body over the treasure.

That's why we couldn't mek out no more 'an four men goin' back when five come ashore. Them four men murdered the fifth one, an' in so doin' enchanted the treasure.

It wuz sealed in human blood, an' the devil himself wuz thar in full charge. An' that's why thunder an' lightnin' comes, an' spectres is seen, an' the treasure sinks lower an' lower, an' the hole caves, when people hev tried to dig up enchanted treasure. An' that's why, too, so little buried treasure hez ever been found, 'cause

pirates mos' al'ays enchant it, an' sometimes enchant it double. They murder
their pris'ners, an' bury 'em, knife in hand,
settin' on the treasure to guard it.

# THE MONEY SHIP

SEVENTY years ago two boys, one seven
years old and the other twelve, made a trip
with their father up the Great South Bay.
They had been promised that when it became necessary to land and mend the nets,
they might run across the Beach to the
ocean.

So, one afternoon when the nets were
spread, away the boys scampered, dragging
their outstretched hands through the tall
grass. But coming upon a damp spot of
meadow when a third of the way over, they
were obliged to turn their course. In doing
so, they chanced to look behind them, and
seeing how far they were from the boat
and how small it appeared, they were

afraid, and had half a mind to turn back.
But the younger lad caught sight of the
large, leafy stalks of a great rose mallow,
a few steps ahead, spreading the broad
petals of its passionate flower out to the
sun and the breeze.

"See them big flowers," he said, to his
brother.

Forgetting their fear, both ran to the
spot, plucked a handful, and continued their
way to the ocean.

"They ain't got any smell," said the
older, "but they're a pretty color."

"Let's get a lot when we come back, and
take 'em home," suggested the younger.

But the showy flowers, deprived of the
abundant moisture which their roots continually send up, soon wilted and lost their
fresh, tropical beauty. Surprised and disappointed at this, the lads threw them
down and quickened their steps. So anxious were they to get across, that the Beach
seemed much wider than they had ever
imagined. At last they reached the ridge

of hills that lie on the inner side of the surf strand, shutting out all view of the ocean, and toiled to the top. The hills seemed very steep and high to them, for in all their lives they had never been away from the low and level south side of the Island.

Reaching the top, that far and mighty prospect of the great deep burst upon them. It was a sight they had expected to see, but a sight of whose accompanying grandeur they had not formed the least conception. They stood silent, each for the time unconscious of the other, while the feeling which comes in the presence of the sublime surged up within their minds.

Young hearts, though, do not give themselves up long to such emotions, and wear their freshness out with pondering, as older people do. With these boys, the spell was brief; but during it the great sea had breathed its infinite benediction upon them, arousing within them feelings unstirred before. The usual traits of boyhood, however, soon asserted themselves, and the boys ran down the slope and began to gather shells and skim them into the surf. They did not, though, whirl away every shell, but, now and then, thrust a pretty one into their pockets. And with the shells they often saved smooth white stones that had been bathed and polished by the sea.

Tiring of this play, they turned to making marks and figures, and writing their names in the wet sand. Then they threw themselves down and dug holes in the wet sand with " skimmauge " shells, and banked the sand up over their feet and hands.

" I wonder where that ship's going and how far away she is ?" said the younger lad.

"Oh, fifty miles—for you can't see anything but her sails, and only a little of them," answered the other.

Then the younger asked if that wasn't the end of the world where the sky went down into the ocean. And watching the

low clouds that floated along the distant
horizon, he fancied that they were going
off to the end of the world.

"May be," he spoke, "they're going
after rain—clouds have some place where
they keep their rain. How slow they're
going! When they get the rain, they'll
hurry back. Why, then they almost fly.
Ain't you seen 'em fly on a stormy day

when they're low aown, and you could
almost see through 'em? I guess they
hurry to scatter the rain over more
ground."

The elder brother paid no heed to these
fancies, but began to roll his trousers up

above his knees as high as he could pull them. The younger quickly did the same, for there were no shoes and stockings to be removed, as bay-men's boys, in those days, went barefooted in summer time.

Then they played along the strand, running down as the waves withdrew from the shore, and as one broke again, and reached up rapidly with its liquid hands, they would run from it. At length, a wave stretched its foamy arms farther up, and caught them ankle deep. The charm of playing with the watery being was broken, and now they waded down, standing knee-deep to feel themselves settle as the undertow scurried past them with its freight of sand. At last, a larger wave came unawares, and wet the elder brother's trousers, changing quickly the current of his thoughts.

"Come," said he, "father told us not to stay over here long. We must hurry right back."

They ran westward to a low spot between the hills, and turned through this pass. As they were following the winding around the edge of a hill, suddenly the older brother grasped the younger's arm, and stopped short before a spot where no grass grew—a slight hollow swept out by the winds.

"See them bones!" he exclaimed. "They're men's bones. There's a hand—

and over there's a skull. See it rock! See it! I'm afraid. Let's run."

Away they ran in their fright, coming out of breath to their father, and telling him with much gasping what they had seen.

"Well," he replied," before we get under-way for home this afternoon, I'll go with you and see what it was. Let me think.

This is near the Old House. It's easy
enough to account for the bones over
there; but the skull's rocking—I guess
you imagined that."

" No, sir, father, I saw it go just like
this—first one side and then the other," replied the elder son, as he suggested the
rocking by the motion of his hands.

"The skull don't rock now," said the
father, when they reached the spot in the
afternoon.   He picked up the skull, and
looking in, saw that a meadow mouse had
built its nest there.

" Yes, boys, I guess you were right.   I've
no doubt now it did rock."

And looking again at the skull, he saw
that there were double teeth all around on
each jaw.   A horror ran through him at
the thought.   He cast the skull away, and
turned to leave the spot, taking his boys by
the hand.   Half-way to the boat he spoke,
saying: " That was a pirate's skull and
them was pirates' bones.   I heard when we

first moved up to this part of the Island
something about pirates being buried
over on the Beach. This must be the
place. I never inquired into the partic'-
lars. I don't like such things, and don't
want to know 'bout 'em. If you do, wait
till you get older, and then inquire into it.
It's bad for you to know such things now."

The incident of coming upon the moving
skull made so profound an impression upon
the elder lad that his curiosity got the
better of him, and in less than two days
after reaching home, he had found someone who knew about what actually had
taken place where the scattered bones lay,
and who, moreover, directed him for fuller
information to old Captain Terry. It was
several years, though, before the lad really
set about further inquiry, there being circumstances which wrought seriously against
it. In the first place, Captain Terry lived
several miles distant, and had the lad
walked up to see him, there was the possibility of his being away from home, or it

at home, too busy to answer the questions of an inquisitive boy. A walk of ten miles to Captain Terry's and back would deter most boys of their curiosity. Then, too, the walk demanded no little courage of a boy who must go alone, or at best, with some companion of his own age ; and should they be detained, causing a return after dark, there were to be passed one or two places along the road of such repute that a boy underwent an ordeal in his own mind in passing them, even in broad daylight.

Clam-Hollow, deep, damp, and dismal, the narrow, crooked road, wooded closely by tall and sombre pines, all interwoven with their thick underbrush, was the scene of many a marvelous happening, which neighborhood talk attributed to that locality; while Brewster's brook, near which the slave murdered his oppressive master, exercised a still stronger influence of fear and horror over the mind of every boy who had ever been past it.

But when the youth had grown towards manhood, and had forgotten the foolish fears and apprehensions of boyhood, when he was doing what he could to make his way in life—sometimes a laborer on farms, sometimes a boatman on the Bay — he heard, at casual times and places, so many allusions and fragmentary accounts of the buccaneers whose bodies lay buried westward of the Old House, that he was led to make full inquiry, and to get at the truth as near as might be. Not only was old Captain Terry's recital heard, but all information that threw any light upon the tragedy was gleaned and treasured, and when an old man he related the following:

Very early in the present century, a ship hove to off Montauk, and set ashore a man.

She had, doubtless, made her landfall near the Inlet, had skirted the coast eastward, attracting no attention whatever—unlike in this respect the ship that the two brothers who went on the Beach "horse-footing" that June Sunday saw anchor close in, send her yawl ashore, and bury treasure, spilling human blood upon it in the act.

When the landing was made the ship stood out to sea and made long tacks off and on, gradually working westward along the coast.

The sailor set ashore was a man of tall and powerful frame. He brought apparently nothing ashore with him, and no sooner had he gained the dry strand than he set out at a brisk pace, making his way westward over the narrow and rocky peninsula. When half the distance to Napeague Beach, he stopped near a large rock and made certain observations. This done, he signalled to the ship, and was answered by the clewing up of the foresail. Then he recommenced his walk towards the village of Amagansette. It was dusk when he reached that village, and his first move was to find where he could spend the night. His applications for lodgings were repeatedly refused by the inhabitants, and that evening and for a week thereafter, the most prominent topic of village talk and conjecture was the stranger who had sought lodgings at so many doors.

Where he passed the night is not known. But the next day, at East Hampton and at South Hampton, the question was frequently asked, " Did you see the stranger that went through the village this morning ? "

Perhaps no ordinary event in those days would have attracted more attention at these villages than the appearance and disappearance of an unknown man. Who he was, what his errand might be, where he came from, and whither he went, were matters of speculation for days; and in this instance there was an additional incentive to curiosity, for the stranger's dress showed him to be a sailor, his manner was rough, his face was cruel in expression, and he held no further word of conversation than was barely necessary to supply his wants.

It is said that after leaving these villages

the stranger was seen making observations on the coast somewhere below Ketchabon-ack. Of his journey westward, nothing more is known, until he was passing over that long, sandy, and solitary tract of road which lies between Forge River and The Mills. Here he stopped, and made some inquiry of Mr. Payne, an old soldier of the Revolution.

When the stranger departed, the family at once asked, " Who was he ? "

The reply made by old Mr. Payne was significant. " That I can't tell; but one thing I can—whoever he is, he has been in human slaughter."

At one of those villages where the Great South Bay broadens to a width of four or five miles, this man was set across to the Beach. To some of the residents there-about he was known, and so, moreover, was the fact that, for a long period, he had been away from home—*piloting*, it was re-ported. His wife and also his daughter, a young woman of defiant mien, saucy speech, and, it is said, of unwholesome reputation, dwelt alone upon the Beach, at what from early colonial days had been called the Old House, but which, since the tragedy of that awful night, has more frequently borne the name of the iniquitous family.

For two days the ship had been sailing east and west, standing off and on shore, awaiting intelligence from him. He saw her the morning he landed on the Beach, but could not signal, as the man who set him across did not return at once. Then, too, after he had gone, two vessels loaded for New York passed within an hour and a half of each other, on their way to Fire Island. Late in the afternoon—the earliest moment he deemed safe—he signalled to the ship that he had reached the spot where all had agreed to land, that circumstances and surroundings were opportune for their purpose, and to hold in position as best possible till darkness settled.

All, however, was not favorable. There were indications of an approaching storm

— indications that portended its sudden approach. The swell on shore, too, was rising and rolling in with stronger volume. They were in a bad position, and well they knew it. There was not sea-room enough, with a south-easterly storm, in that angle of the coast. But what cared that reckless crew now about their ship, other than she must not go ashore within sight or reach of where they proposed to land.

Night came, and a fire flamed up on the shore, built low down near the tide mark, that the hills might hide all view of it from people upon the main-land. It was the signal when to leave ship and where to come ashore. According to the understanding on ship-board off Montauk, the fire was to be set three rods westward of the best spot of beach to land, within half a mile of the Old House.

There was hurry on ship-board. Time pressed, for the edges of the storm were upon them. Two of the ship's yawls were lowered, made fast alongside, and into these were passed canvas bags, containing coin and, it is supposed, other valuables. Each member of the crew had secured in some manner upon his person his own share of the results of their hazardous and wicked doings. When the yawls were ready, the crew made efforts to scuttle the ship, so that she might sink during the night. But, doubtless owing to the haste imposed by the coming storm, these efforts did not promise success; and fearing that the vessel, when abandoned, would be driven directly ashore, orders were given to take in part of the sail, leaving in trim just spread of canvas enough to keep the ship in the wind. Then, heading her seaward and lashing the helm to windward, the buccaneers embarked in the yawls and pulled towards shore—seventeen men in all, abandoning a life of robbery and murder, but bringing with them the booty such a life had secured.

Nearing the shore, they saw by the firelight the form of their accomplice. No

other man was with him, and yet the forms
of two other persons were seen in the circle of light which the fire radiated out into
the dark. There was shouting to and fro
of how to come on, and oaths and harsh
accusations besides—why he had been so
long, and why had he signalled them on
when a storm was already in the rigging.
The surf was threatening, but it was too
late now to make any other decision.
With strength of oar they held themselves
in position, watching the right moment to
take the best wave and ride in. But
whether directions were misunderstood, or
whether in the darkness there was miscal-
culation, the yawls swamped upon the bar,
throwing the seventeen buccaneers into
the rushing surf. It was a despairing, mad
struggle for life, with piercing cries and
blasphemy heard above the booming of the
waves. Two buccaneers, Tom Knight and
Jack Sloane, gained the shore. Others
sank soon, while yet others, quite exhausted, might have been rescued. But

treachery, calculating its chance, stepped in and did foul work. Then what horrible exertion went on all that night! What hot search was kept up for lifeless forms as the sea tossed them up! How, when discovered, were they pulled out of the edge of the surf, and clothing rifled! And then, to cover it all, their bodies were dragged to a hollow among the hills, and there buried. The storm set in before the night was half gone, and a wild day followed, keeping from the Beach any boatman that chance might have led that way.

Tom Knight and Jack Sloane, not a fortnight thereafter, made their appearance upon the main shore, and spent money freely. They came and went, again and again, always spending with the same lavish hand, throwing down, it is said, a Spanish dollar for the most trivial purchase, and invariably refusing any change.

Rumors that some horrid deed had been committed were soon in circulation, and conjectures of what had happened upon the Beach were many and various.

A town magistrate, hearing these, began an inquiry. He sent constables to the Beach with warrants to arrest the family and everyone else in the house. Only the mother and the daughter were found. These were brought to the main-land, and half a day was spent in examination; but the magistrate could find no positive evidence that warranted further action on his part.

On the day the mother and daughter were arrested, those three buccaneers—the pilot, Tom Knight, and Jack Sloane— watched from hiding-places apart in the hills, the coming and going of the constables. When all possibility of detection had passed, they returned to the Old House. Each sought out his treasure whence he had temporarily hid it, in the bushes or in the sand. After hot discussion, each packed his gold according to his own notion, and the three buccaneers struggled through the hills in separate directions to bury their treasure.

Tom Knight's gold was found forty years after, just as he had sealed it up in the black pot which the Captain found, in that last fortunate patrol of the Beach; the gold of the other buccaneers lies somewhere among those sand-hills until this day.

Immediately after the arrest, Tom Knight and Jack Sloane left for other parts, and very shortly the family broke up its residence on the Beach and moved to the Western frontier, where, it is said, ill-fate and disaster followed them.

That portion of the Beach, however, attracted many thither. But little money was then in circulation. The government, it was well known, had coined money but a few years, while Spain was imagined to have stamped untold millions; and the hope of finding Spanish coin quickly sprang up in many a man's mind. In consequence, bay-men often strolled along that part of the coast, though most of them took good heed not to be there after dark. Spanish dollars were frequently found—one person picking up first and last thirty-eight of these. Search was even made upon the bar where the yawls upset. But periods when the sea was smooth enough to work were rare, and what is more, the exact spot was unknown. Fragments of the canvas bags were found, and a few coins; but nothing commensurate to expectation and the time spent in search.

The ship remained off the coast, and as if guided by an insane pilot, alternately sailed and drifted, veering her course through every point of the compass from northeast to southeast, but working, singularly enough, all the time eastward.

Her strange behavior attracted one day the attention of a party of fishermen on the Beach opposite Smith's Point. Some of them proposed most ardently that the surf-boat be launched and the ship boarded. But others of them were afraid, and stoutly opposed any such adventure. And so a prize of more value than the catch of many seasons passed them, because, let us say it plainly, superstition was stronger than reason.

Near South Hampton the Money Ship went ashore. There were neither papers nor cargo on board which would indicate where she came from. A sea-merchant thought some of the casks that were found in the hold had contained Italian silks. Seven Spanish doubloons were found on a locker in the cabin, and several cutlasses and pistols were scattered about. The whole vessel was searched, but nothing more could be found. Two of those men, though, who had aided in the search went on board at nightfall. Suddenly, while peering about, their light went out, and one man, frightened and deaf to persuasion, fled ashore. The other, undaunted, made anew his light and continued the

search. While hunting about the cabin, he bethought to pry away a part of the ceiling. Upon doing so, he found a quantity of money concealed there, and as it dropped down from its place of lodgment.

some of the coins rolled out of the cabin-window into the sea. This time it was an honest man's treasure, and he carried ashore that night many a hatful. Just how much was thus secured could never be learned. Some put the amount at two hundred dollars, others, and by far the greater number, thought it many times this sum. One thing is certain—there were marked changes noticeable in the circumstances of that family from that time, and the signs of prosperity were not only sudden but lasting.

Whence came the Money-Ship? There was not even a name or commission to give any clew. Could she have been an English merchantman, which had chanced to be in the West Indies during the insurrection in Hayti, and on board of which some of the French inhabitants of the island had sought refuge, bringing with them their wealth,—that when at sea, mutiny had arisen, the officers and passengers had been made way with, and their wealth appropriated by the sailors ?

Was she a Spanish pirate from the Gulf, with half her crew English sailors ?

Or was she a galleon sailing from the Spanish main to old Spain ?

It has always remained a mystery.

"WESTWARD OF GREEN'S BROOK"

# WIDOW MOLLY

WESTWARD of Greene's brook on the road to Oakdale there stands a substantial country residence. You will recognize it in driving by, for just south, across the road is a lot with small spindle cedars growing all irregular, everywhere in fact, some perhaps the height of a man's waist, but the most not higher than his knee.

"Poor land," you will say. Well, I believe it is. Else why are those little wizened cedars there? They have grown there who knows how long? They never get bigger, and have each the appearance, when you come close, of being a hundred years old. But the lot with them on, bends its mile of curve gradually down to the Great South Bay, and leaves you a broad view of that body of water, very blue and very beautiful at times.

A century and nine years ago, there stood across the road opposite this lot a small inn. At what time it was demolished, I could never learn; but I have no doubt some of its wrecked timbers are doing upright duty to this very day, in bracing the partitions of the present residence.

Sometimes the New York stage stopped at this inn, but its usual halting-place was a few miles to the west at Champlin's. Whenever it did stop, the passengers had good cheer, for the little inn was kept by Widow Molly—a woman of sunny face and hopeful disposition.

Her eyes were large, and, you would say, a little too deeply placed; but their look was honest and as unsuspecting as the stars. She had broad hips of which she was a trifle proud, a round arm and a very pretty hand, a deep chest, arching high, and her weight must have been not more than a pound or two either side of one hundred and sixty.

There was no end of trooping in those days, and many a company of horsemen stopped at Widow Molly's. Her slave, Ebo, would give the best care to the horses, while she entertained their riders. And if the troopers had time and it came to a game of seven-up, she could play as strong a hand as any one of them. The hours on such halts went too fast, and often afterwards there was hard riding to regain time lost lingering. But of all the riders who dismounted at her door, there was one who came alone and went alone, and whose visits were beginning to hint of regularity. He came from the section about

Ronkonkoma Pond, seven miles, perhaps, to the northward. Whoever knew him, knew him as the young squire. Seven-and-thirty years old, prosperous, of sound judgment, he well deserved the note the office gave him.

In the spring that came a century and nine years ago, the young squire, who had always a passion for cracking away at stray ducks that settled in the Pond, resolved to go gunning to the "South Side." And many a morning or afternoon he lay behind the cedars that grew along the shore of the Great South Bay, and tolled in ducks, by flapping over his head a piece of bright red flannel tied to his ramrod. On these gunning expeditions he always stopped at the inn, and finally, instead of carrying his firelock home, he left it in the keeping of Widow Molly. The hostess stood the gun in the corner of the front room.

Whenever the young squire came, he found the brass upon it bright and the

stock and barrel rubbed off with a mite of
oil. Widow Molly did this with her own
hands, and never made mention of it. But
one day, when he took his gun to start for
the shore, he gave one deep look into her
eyes and kissed her as he passed out of the
doorway. She watched him go across the
lot till the curve put him out of sight, and
then turning, closed the door. It was well
that during the rest of that day no one
halted at the inn desiring refreshment, for
the genial hostess would have seemed to
such, preoccupied. From the moment she
turned from that wrapt watching in the
doorway, she wandered off with the feelings of her heart whither neither guest
nor friend could follow and intrude.

That afternoon, when the day's gunning
was over, the squire was met by a neighbor and summoned home to write the will
of a dying man. He had not time so
much as to enter the house, but gave his
gun and four brace of ducks to Ebo, and

rode rapidly home with the neighbor who had come for him.

After tea, when Judy was washing the dishes, Widow Molly came into the kitchen with the gun, laid it down upon the table, and began cleaning it. This time she even drew the ramrod, wound a rag around it, and wiped out the barrel. When she had put it in perfect order, she carried it into the front room and stood it in its usual corner.

" Law," said Judy to Ebo, as they sat in the kitchen by the scant light of one tallow dip, " what am got into missus ? Di' jou see how she clean dat ere gun so' ticlar to-night ? She am done it sivral time afore, but nebber so drefful 'ticlar ez to-night. An' the squar am no stop to-night! Wha' for he din't stay to tea an' spen' ebnin' wi' missus? Missus am dispinted; drefful so.

" We'se goin' to lose Missus, dat am sure, cause I'se kin *feel* it. Missus been kinde way off, thinkin' an' thinkin' to herself all

long back.   Yes,  we'se  goin'  to  lose
Missus, an' whar's poor ol' Judy goin' in
dese ere war  times ?—Ebo, you fas' asleep
dar ?   Git off to yer own quarters."

In that spring, a century and nine years
ago, a schooner, manned by outlaws prin-
cipally from the Connecticut shore, but
some, be it said, from the south side of the
Island, made her appearance in the Bay.
She would come in Fire Island Inlet,

course eastward up the Bay, robbing every vessel within reach ; and in the spirit of pure devilment, the crew would destroy or cut adrift every boat they robbed, set their owners ashore on the Beach at whatever point most convenient, and then slip out of the inlet near the Manor of St. George, and be gone.

One or two visits of this sort put baymen upon their guard, and when the stranger hove in sight, it was crack on all sail, and make for shallow water or disappear up some creek or river.

Finding their opportunities of robbing upon the Bay at an end, the outlaws determined to take to land. The scattered residents, expecting it would come to this, had organized a sort of company who should be ready at the briefest notice to repel any such attempts.

Again the schooner appeared in the Bay, sailed eastward, and anchored off the mouth of Great River. The news of her approach spread rapidly, and a part of the

company quickly gathered and took a concealed place behind a bunch of cedars on
the shore to watch any movements that
might be made from the schooner.    After
sunset they saw a boat lowered and
manned.

At the foot of the lot on which the
cedars now grow there was a landing-place.
The men on shore saw the yawl push out
from the schooner and head towards the
landing.

They watched ten minutes, and the yawl
did not change its course.

"Some man in that yawl knows well
enough where this landing-place is, an'
they're coming to it, you can bet your last
guinea," remarked Jim Avery.  "My ad-
vice is to git away from here quick, an'
take to the lime-kiln."

"Wait a few minutes first, to make sure
they're comin'," suggested someone.

They watched five minutes longer, and
then, keeping a thick bunch of cedars
directly in range of the boat. they ran half-

bent to the lime-kiln and shell-heap at the landing, and there concealing themselves, set one of their number to watch the movements of the boat.

In the lime-kiln they began to discuss a plan of action.

" Load the big musket with buckshot and give that to 'em first, if they undertake to land," was the first proposition.

" Put in a rippin' good charge. Four fingers of powder, and ram it hard"—added Jim Avery.

The steel ramrod sent out its cling as the wad was pounded down.

" Oh, the devil ! Put in more buckshot than that if you want 'em to know we mean it. There ! " continued Jim, as he clapped his hand over the bore and let a handful of buckshot guzzle down upon the first charge, " that'll plug 'em."

After the big gun was loaded the men began to load their own guns, their excitement increasing and the discussion growing loud enough to be heard outside the

kiln. At length, the natural leader of
the party checked it, and fixed a plan of
action.

" 'The thing to do," he said, "is this: hail
'em when they get near the shore, an' if
they don't hold up, rip into 'em a volley
from the big gun, an' hold our other fire-
locks in resarve."

But a question at once arose who should
fire the big musket. It required a stout
man to hold the huge firearm out, and the
smallest man of the group, in the haste of
gathering, had caught it up in a neighbor's
house.

" I swar I won't fire it with such a load
as that in," he said; "and I can't fire it
anyway without a rest."

" You take her, then," said the leader to
one who stood beside him.

" Not a bit of it. I ain't agoin' to fire
nobody else's gun but my own."

" They're not more'n three gun-shots
off," spoke the sentinel, husking the tones
of his voice; "settle upon suthin' darn

quick, ur we'll hev a han'-to-han' fight here
on the shore."

"You're the boy, Jim; you fire it," said
the leader, clapping a negro who stood near
him, on the shoulder.

Jim took the gun.

It was now dusk. The party slipped out
from behind the shell-heap, and the leader
shouted, "Back water there an' stop, or
I'll fire."

No reply was made, but he caught
the words, "Pull, *pull*;" and the quicker
dip of the oars told that the rowers
heeded.

" Another yard and I'll fire."

No word of reply—but, spoken loud and with vengeance, " Pull, damn you, *pull*."

" Fire, Jim; " and the huge musket thundered out her volley.

A shriek from one poor devil, the noise of others falling over in the boat, and the striking of oars followed. With oaths and confusion, the outlaws turned their boat and pulled back.

Black Jim stood stiff in the tracks where he had fired, but the big musket lay upon the ground—the recoil had broken his collar-bone.

In the morning the schooner was gone. Week after week went by, and the scattered inhabitants continually expected some descent of the outlaws to take vengeance for their repulse. Jim's collar-bone was well knit together, and yet there had been no further molestation.

" I guess we fixed 'em. They don't seem to want to come any more," remarked one of the party to a neighbor.

More than six weeks had passed since that one charge of buckshot repulsed the outlaws, and June was half gone. The Bay's rest spell was come—the time when, day after day, its surface is calm, and the air above it quivers—the time when the Beach goes off to its farthest limit and melts into islands with air inlets between them.

On one of those quiet, dreamy days in June, when all thought of alarm is farthest from one, the identical long-boat which barely two months before had turned back with its wounded, was crossing the Bay, and making, too, directly for the landing by the lime-kiln and shell-heap. The schooner this time lay outside the Beach, and the outlaws had made a portage over with their long-boat. Again someone in that boat knew there was a landing near the shell-heap.

They rowed up till the boat touched the sand, but before all landed, two sailors jumped ashore and went around the shell-heap and into the kiln to discover whether any body of men was lying in wait there. Upon their return, the boat was secured, and the oars were put in position for quick launching. Then, adjusting slashed black bands across their faces, the outlaws took their way up across the lot, making straight for the inn on the north side of the old country road. A dozen rods, perhaps, from the shore, there sprang up what always springs up when any group of sailors take to land —what in general may be called rough fooling. It was started by Nate Crosby, the most irrepressible devil of the whole crew, throwing his leg between those of the sailor who walked beside him, and sending him sprawling to the ground, his face tearing into one of the stunted cedars. As he rose, he plucked the cedar up, and began lashing Nate about the neck and face, and not only did he deal blows at Nate, but also upon those who laughed at the way Nate had thrown him. Whereupon some five or six others uprooted cedars and fell to cracking back, and then at each other.

"What in thunder are you thinking of, you devil's birds?" said the leader, stepping back among them. "Quit this fooling. We're darn near in sight of the inn, and instead of keeping your eyes skinned for just what some of us got the last time we tried this thing, you've taken to rollicking. Spread out, spread out; don't bunch up, if you've got any wit whatever. Nate, cast away that cedar; cast it away, and come with me to the head of the gang."

They reached the inn and filed into the front room. There was no one at home but Widow Molly and Judy, and both were at work in the kitchen. The noise and boisterous talk brought Widow Molly to the room in an instant, and Judy, taking one peep, scrambled down cellar and hid herself in a bin.

"Ah! Dame Molly," said the leader very affably, as she entered, "a surprise to you! What of cheer can ye make us?"

"Mek it damn quick, too," broke in a rough voice.

"Hold your jaw, you ill-trained cur," spoke the leader, smiting the upstart flat-handed on the mouth.

Such words, the black bands with fierce eyes looking through, the knives and pistols thrust in their belts, told Widow Molly that the gang of outlaws had landed and were in her house. The thought that she was alone came swift, and she stood a moment stricken and dazed. But quite as suddenly she regained her self-possession, stepped past them into an adjoining room, reached a decanter and glasses, and setting these before them, bade them drink their pleasure.

"More, *more*," thundered one outlaw, hammering on the table with the butt of his pistol.

She brought another decanter and glasses. The two decanters were emptied, refilled, and emptied again before the outlaws gave heed to anything else.

" And now, Dame Molly, thou hast well slaked our thirst, can'st thou not bring something to stay our stomachs," said the leader.

" An' bring thy silver spoons, too," said another of the company, who, turning towards her, chucked her under the chin.

Her eyes flashed with resentment at the indignity, and swifty she whirled a stinging slap in the intruder's face.

A roar of laughter filled the room, and derisively they cried, " Try it ag'in, now, will ye ?  Try it ag'in."

Widow Molly's heart beat hard.  Her breath was catchy, and with her capacious lungs that was a new experience.  A way of escape was her first thought.  Should she slip out of the kitchen door, run a mile to the nearest neighbor, and give the alarm ?

She found no chance to do it, for three of the outlaws followed her into the pantry and then into the kitchen.  Nothing was left but to put on the bravest appearance,

and she had already done that.  Had they
been soldiers with  muskets, their presence
would not have affected her as it did.  She
was  used  to  muskets.  But  the  dirks,
sheath-knives, and  horse-pistols that filled
their belts gave her a tremor.

Everything eatable the inn afforded she
set before them, and although there was
considerable of  it, it  was  not  sufficient to
fill  them  all.  During  the  whole  while,
Widow  Molly  waited  on  the  ravenous
crowd, and  when  the  eating  came  to an
end, the  leader said, "And  now, Dame
Molly, produce thy purse and what of gold
thou hast besides."  She drew forth her
purse and emptied it upon the table.  A
sailor started towards the table and made a
grab, but he was caught by the leader, and
shoved back against the wall with a thud.

"Four pound ten," said the leader, count-
ing it; "and that's all ye have about, Dame
Molly?  Search  the  house  from  garret  to
cellar.  Hold—two stay in the room with
our landlady."

Forth they burst into all parts of the house, striding up stairs, kicking open doors instead of unlatching them. Clatter and din came from every room. Beds were upturned, drawers ransacked and the contents turned upon' the floor, looked over, and then kicked into corners to make room for other examinations. Closets were rummaged, feather-beds and pillows thrown upon the floor, felt over carefully, and then as carefully trodden over, to make sure nothing was concealed therein.

" Look for loose bricks in the fireplaces. See if the hearth-stones are tight down," shouted the leader, from the head of the stairs.

And with these words, Widow Molly heard Judy's cries from the cellar imploring mercy from the outlaw who was hustling her about and demanding where the silver was.

"Oh, please, sah, lem me go. Don't. Oh! oh! don't."

" No, sah; no, sah; true es I lib, missus ain't got no silber."

"Oh, dear, hab marcy, please, sah; do hab marcy. Oh, *oh!* — — — you break my poor ol' arm."

" Fall on yer knees. Stop your beggin' for mercy."

" Yes, sah; *yes, sah.* Hab a little marcy. Oh !— — —."

" Clasp yer hands above yer head. Keep 'em up there."

" Oh, sah, *oh !*— — —"

" Stop yer beggin'. Another whimper and I'll pull. Now, you tell quick, where the silver is, or I'll blow your old black head into mince-meat."

Judy, shaking with fear, told him.

The outlaw came up out of the cellar, and rummaged where Judy had said. Securing several small pieces of silver-ware, he came back into the front room. Then for the first time he noticed the gun, with its bright mountings, which stood in

the corner, and walking towards it, he remarked, " That gun's mine."

" No," replied Widow Molly, her affec-
tion rising as she thought of him to whom
the gun belonged. " You can have anything else. That's a friend's gun."

He took it, and Widow Molly, who had
already stepped across the room, seized the
gun, and with one strong, quick twist,
wrested it from him. Setting it back in
the corner, she replied, " That you can't
have as long as I can defend it."

One of the outlaws who had been keeping her prisoner now tried the same game.

All the woman's soul again stirred within her. She wrested the gun from him, but the struggle was hard and long.

"I tell you," she said, as she fell back with the gun in her possession—"I tell you," she repeated between breaths, "that's a friend's gun, and I'll defend it. You can't have it."

Then with the gun in her hand she walked directly across the room into an adjoining one, and set the gun behind the door.

In the meantime the leader passed from room to room to see what valuables had been found. The outlaws put into their pockets a few nondescript articles that struck their fancy, but nothing of any great value, and they had searched through everything. For some time there had been cursing at their want of luck, but now that it had become disappointment, their blasphemy was frightful. The whole gang came tramping down the stairs, swearing and threatening in ugly mood, and filed into the front room. Widow Molly, who stood at the farthest side, grew deathly white.

They will now, thought she, resort to some desperate scheme. She took a long, deep breath, and then caught it to stop the flutter of her bosom. "And no one comes!" she almost said aloud in her emotion.

All through the time of their ransacking, she had felt that they would be surprised in their robbery by a company of the townsmen, or that, perchance, some body of horsemen would ride up. Now that hope was wholly gone.

But shouts came from two outlaws in the garret who had been reaching down behind the rafters.

"Gold—gold!" they shouted. "We've found it. We ain't *clean* dished."

The outlaws in the front room surged into the hall, and yelled as the finders came jumping down-stairs. The group at the foot of the stairs stood back to give passage, and the finders rushed through into the front room, followed eagerly by the crowd.

Nate Crosby threw upon the table a stout, heavily-filled stocking, drew his sheath-knife, severed the stocking just below where it was tied, and poured the contents out upon the table,

"Stand back," said the leader, "whilst I count and divide."

The group very willingly stood back, formed a circle about the table, and grinned and chuckled as the coins were counted.

"One hundred and eighty pounds, all told."

The leader counted out a pile to each man, setting up the coins as he did so. And when this was done, he handed each man his pile. "The other booty," he said, "goes into the common lot."

"And now, my rovers," continued the leader, "no more marauding for this day. Back to our boat, forthwith."

"Good-day, Dame Molly. Your hospitality has been right well enjoyed;" and hurrying out of the house, the outlaws struck into a run for the landing.

Widow Molly sank into a chair, and let her arms fall beside her in an exhausted way. After a brief space she summoned energy sufficient to go to the window and assure herself that they were not returning. She was just in time to see them disappear below the curve of the cedar lot. One outlaw at the rear, she noticed, carried a gun. She turned swiftly and went into the adjoining room to see whether the gun had been taken from behind the door. It was gone. Then Widow Molly buried her face in her hands and cried bitterly.

"Devil Dan'l showed that gang the way, you may be sartin'. Who else 'ud know the place and Widow Molly's name?" was the common remark from Swan River to Penataquit.

The feeling against the outlaws was intense, and a company of men from five leagues along the South Road was organized to be ready at courier's summons.

For a few days the schooner's masts were seen outside the Beach, coursing one day westward, and the next eastward—lingering for some purpose off the coast.

Another descent was expected, and the inhabitants conjectured it would be made during the night. Squads of five or six men patrolled their neighborhoods, with horses ready to summon other squads in any emergency.

On the fourth night, the scattered guard-groups noticed, early in the evening, the low beat of the surf upon the Beach. In the course of the night it grew stronger, and the pounding of each huge breaker could be distinctly told.

In those days every man was a weather-prophet, and every man awake that night said, " There's a big storm off at sea, and we'll likely get it here."

The next day broke with a dull sky and a

raw east wind that betokened the coming of the storm. The wind rose as the day progressed, and mid-afternoon a few drops of rain—the harbingers of the storm—showed themselves upon the window-panes. At that very hour, the schooner, low-reefed, was seen close in under the Beach, scudding westward. It was evident to those who saw her that she was making for some near harbor.

The night came wild and wet. The wind blew great rushing sweeps from the south-east, crowding the water up into the western part of the Bay, forcing it up creeks and over meadows. Between midnight and morning, the wind suddenly shifted into the west, like the banging of a door, and blew with just as great fury. The whole black area of clouds and rain bore back from the west. The gulls alone found life in it.

In three hours the wind wore itself out, but there followed a thick morning, with the Bay and the sky all one wet blend of gray.

At noon the dampness lifted, and the Beach showed itself.

Keen eyes were not long in discerning, as they scanned it, two masts and a hull, heeled over. The schooner was ashore—inside the Beach at the Point of Woods.

Scudding west the afternoon before, and now ashore at the Point of Woods and heeled over! What was the inference from the two things? Plainly to every inhabitant, that the outlaws had run the schooner into Fire Island for a harbor, and when the wind made that sudden shift, the vessel had fouled anchor or parted chain and had gone ashore.

That afternoon there was brisk riding to summon the squads of men.

"Now's our chance, if ever. They'll hang on there till high tide 'bout midnight, an' try to get 'er off. But they won't find as much water piled up there agin at high tide as they went ashore in. An' to-mor-row, after workin' an' tuggin' half the night to no purpose, they'll conclude to abandon her," were the rousing words of a man who gathered a small squad, at Islip within half an hour after the word of summons came.

By understanding, the place of rendezvous was the old tavern still standing at Blue Point, where the road running south makes a sharp angle and bends to the west.

Two squads came from the west—twelve men. They halted at Widow Molly's, and rested a short time in that front room. They talked of the ransacking and robbery of the house, and nothing else; boasted of the vengeance they would take out of those "hell-birds;" drank two or three times around, and then set out for Blue Point, assuring the hostess that they would recover her gold.

Widow Molly made no reply to this, but to Captain Ben of the Penataquit squad, with whom she walked to the door, she said quietly, " Bring back, if nothing else, a gun with brass mountings, which they took the last thing without my knowing it. It must be on board somewhere."

A squad came up from Patchogue, and when those from the west arrived at the tavern, there were twenty-six men ready for the enterprise.

Three hours passed in discussing plans and selecting a leader. It could not have been done in less time. Every man had *his* ideas, and every man had to be heard. And so the company gradually broke up into groups. One knot of men stood outside the tavern door, a group of five or six were out by the barn, a number walked towards the shore to see just the position the schooner lay in, thinking that a sight of her from Blue Point would suggest the best move to make. When those who walked towards the shore came back, they suggested that all go into the tavern and either all agree upon some plan or give the affair up and go home. In all the discussion two or three self-contained men had kept quiet, knowing evidently that there must be just so much futile talk, and that when this had become tiresome, the company would adopt any good plan.

Among those who had said very little was Captain Ben of Penataquit. A little vexed, he suddenly stepped into a chair and spoke: " This talk can go on till Doomsday, but it won't accomplish anything. Now, I know, there has been three or four plans stated; but I propose this as the surest one, though it'll take longer an' be harder on us. After dark, muffle our oars, an' row across the Bay to Long Cove. Land there, draw our boats up an' cover 'em with sea-weed. At midnight start west along the surf-shore, an' when we get opposite to where the schooner is ashore, cross the Beach, an' surprise the crew at daybreak. That's the main plan. All the rest'll have to be decided accordin' to what turns up."

This plan met a hearty reception; and someone forthwith proposed that Captain

Ben be made leader, which was just as heartily agreed to.

It was four miles across to Long Cove, and nearly seven miles down the Beach to where the schooner lay. They took with them such provisions as could be secured, and as soon as twilight had wholly faded, pulled across the Bay. It was past nine o'clock when they made the start, for the days were then at their longest.

They struck the Beach a little east of Long Cove, but followed it up, entered the Cove, and drew their boats up.

" We've got plenty o' time," said Captain Ben, " an' we'd better take a bite o' what we've got afore we start. There's no knowin' when we'll get the next chance."

Standing around the boats or sitting on the gunwales, the men ate and drank and talked. Shortly after midnight they shouldered their arms, crossed the Beach, and began the march westward along the surf shore.

The inner side of the Beach is covered

with marshes and meadows, indented most
irregularly by the Bay. But along the
ocean side there is a smooth piece of
strand, six or eight rods wide, and flanked
all along by steep sand-hills, which sometimes rise thirty feet high. Along this

piece of strand lay their line of march. It
was hard travelling, for the sand, unless
wet, is not firm, but yields under the foot,
and gives forth at every step a creaking
note, doubtless caused by the particles of
salt that are commingled with the sand.

The sounds coming from so many footsteps made one continuous creaking, very much like the sound of a loaded wagon drawn over a snow-packed road.

The surf boomed and pounded, rushed and seethed and swirled, so that thirty rods from the group the noise of their footsteps was swallowed up. The men, though, heard the creaking continually, and it apparently grew louder and more distinct. It seemed to them to be giving the alarm of their coming to the whole Beach.

"I'm goin' to take to the wet sand," said a man in the middle of the group. "I've had enough of this everlastin' creak, creak, creak."

The tide was half-way down, and as he struck for the wet sand, he was followed by the rest of the company. They found the sand firmer, and the walking easier. Now and then a wave would lap up and wet their feet. They were used to wet feet, all of them; but creaking sand at every footstep on a midnight march they could not endure.

When the first streaks of daylight showed themselves in the east, Captain Ben put his followers in file close up under the surf hills. So soon as daylight grew strong enough to define faintly the reaches of the coast, he crept to the top of the row of hills, and reconnoitred the Beach. He could just make out dimly, a mile westward, the masts and hull of the stranded schooner. He backed down from the sandhill and reported what he had seen.

"About a mile to west'ard, an' nobody stirrin' as I can make out. See that your guns are all well primed an' dry. Keep in close to the hills till we get abreast the spot. And now, forward!"

There were two or three places in the hills in that mile, where the ocean had broken through and poured its waters over low spots of beach into the Bay. Cautiously the men skulked by these openings.

"I b'lieve in bein' wary," said a Blue Point bay-man. "There's no calc'latin' what we may run upon any minute—mebbe the hull poss on 'em in some o' these ere hill hollers."

The daylight was now fast flooding ocean and Beach and Bay. What they were to do must be done quickly.

Captain Ben gathered his followers close in under the bank, while he climbed to the top of the sand ridge and peered over. He saw distinctly the masts of the schooner, but not the hull, as the second ridge of hills cut off his view. He slipped back a few yards, and directed the men to range themselves abreast and crawl over the hill into the next valley or, rather, depression between the surf hills and the middle beach range.

When all were over and down, he gave word to crawl on hands and knees up the ridge before them, and to halt within twenty yards of the top, while he again peered over.

The day was now fully open. The creeping line of men came towards the top of the ridge, and Captain Ben waved his hand backwards for them to stop. The line halted, and every man drew himself up on his knees to watch the Captain.

He had crept not three lengths after waving his hand for the line to halt, when, as suddenly and unexpectedly as if some dead sailor had risen from his grave among those Beach hills, a man stepped over the crest of the hill.

In an instant and with one impulse, the Captain, and those in the line behind him, levelled their muskets at the outlaw.

He was startled, but his senses came quick as Captain Ben growled, " Not a breath from you, you devil, or out goes your brains. Drop, an' crawl to rear."

The outlaw dropped upon all fours and crawled to the rear, the men all the while covering him with their muskets.

The moment he reached the line, he was

seized by seven or eight strong hands. Captain Ben was there as quick.

" Gag him.—Not a whimper from you, either! "

The outlaw yielded as he felt a bayonet prick his side and saw a musket lifted above his head ready to stave his skull.

" Bind his hands behind him," continued the Captain.    " Tie his feet—tie his legs above his knees, and muffle him."

Then they tore the outlaw's hat into shreds, and with rough hands stuffed these shreds into his mouth around the gag-stick.

Meanwhile, Captain Ben crept to the top of the hill and peered over.    No one else was stirring on board the schooner.

The outlaw that was now lying at the bottom of the hollow, bound so that he could not move, gagged and so nearly choked that he could give no alarm, was doubtless the last watch, who at daylight, seeing that all was well, had taken it into his head to stroll over to the ocean side, and see what was doing there.

" This devil out of the way and no one else stirring, there is every chance of surprising the outlaws before they turn out," thought Captain Ben.

He, therefore, ordered the men to creep over the hill and down the slope as far as possible, separating all they could in doing so. Then, when he rose, the rest were to follow his example, rush toward the schooner, and board her if possible.

Over they crept and down through the grass, sticking the coarse sedge-stumps into their hands and knees. The time that passed in getting over to the ridge and down to the meadow seemed to them tenfold as long as it really was. They watched the schooner constantly, yet no one was seen stirring on board.

When at last off the slope of the hill and down upon the level meadow, the Captain rose to his feet, and, crouching very low, ran toward the vessel. The others quickly followed his example, all keeping the sharpest eye on the schooner, and ready to fall flat upon the meadow at the least sign of anyone coming on deck.

They were within ten rods of the schooner, when an outlaw, half dressed, stepped out of the cabin gangway. He had just stepped out of his berth, and sailor-like, had come on deck the first thing to look at the weather.

The instant his head popped above the cabin entrance, every man upon the meadow fell flat and watched him.

It was an exciting moment. Though they were lying as close to the ground as possible, there was no rank growth of new grass to conceal them, and had the outlaw cast his eyes upon the meadow where they lay, he would surely have detected their presence.

But although a man is out of his berth, his senses are not at their brightest. He must yawn a little, and stretch himself and clear his throat. All this the outlaw did

his face turned from the Beach and looking out over the Bay.

Captain Ben, seeing this, rose stealthily,
and with one vigorous sweep of his arm,
signalled the men to rush toward the
schooner. There was not a second lost in
obeying. The splash of a dozen men in
the water, who made for the schooner's
bow in order to board her forward, attracted suddenly the outlaw's attention, and
whirling around, he took in at a glance the
whole surprise.

The schooner was harder aground aft,
and lay obliquely, with her stern almost
touching the meadow bank. To this point
Captain Ben and the others of his company
ran, and drew their guns on the outlaw.

"Surrender or I'll pull," shouted Captain
Ben.

"Five minutes to consider," asked the
outlaw, who afterwards proved to be the
leader of the gang.

"Not a second," replied the Captain.
'Speak the word, or you're a dead man."

The men who plunged for the bow of the schooner had now gained the deck, and were rushing for the outlaw, while those on shore kept their guns levelled on him. Two of the stoutest men seized and pinioned him with the main sheet.

The outlaws below, aroused by the noise, rushed up the cabin gangway just as they had sprung from their berths, bareheaded, barefooted, with breeches and shirt on, but suspenders flapping.

When they sprang from their berths, they caught up whatever weapons came first to hand—pistols, dirks, sheath-knives. In their excitement two attempted to come through the gangway at the same time, and one of Captain Ben's men, seeing his advantage, instantly clubbed his musket and struck. The blow hurled both the outlaws back upon those rushing up behind, and thus cleared for a second the gangway stairs. Down rushed the man with a bayonet on his gun, followed by others. A pistol-bullet gouged a piece out of his left arm, but he kept his man at bay. By this time all the rest of the townsmen were on board, and crowded, as many as possible, into the cabin. The fight grew fierce. The cabin became filled with smoke from the shots fired. But there was no chance to reload, and the butt of the musket was used with horrible execution. Blood flowed and bones were broken. The struggle, however, lasted but ten minutes. In that short time most of the outlaws lay stunned upon the cabin floor; the others had been pressed into berths and corners, and pinioned. And so soon as those upon the floor showed any signs of reviving, they were bound strongly. A few irons were found on board, and these were used as far as they would go. The outlaws were put under guard, and given over to some colonial officials, but into just what custody is not now known.

The schooner was searched from stem to stern that very morning, and booty of some value secured. Not a pound, though,

of Widow Molly's gold was brought to
light.   In the cabin, however, in a conspic-
uos place, hung the gun with brass mountings.

And that night the part of the company
that went westward stopped at Widow
Molly's, and Captain Ben handed her the
gun.   The men lingered an hour in the
front room, and drank the hostess' health
again and again.

When they had gone and the house had
become quiet, Widow Molly took her candle
and the gun and went into the kitchen.
She cleaned and polished it, working till
her candle was low in the stick.   Sometimes a tear fell, but they were the tears
that overflow from a bounding heart.

A few evenings after, the young squire
came.   They sat and talked into the quiet
stretches of the evening.   Then Widow
Molly brought him the gun.   As he took
it he kissed her, but not one time only as
at first.   And when the squire carried the

gun home, she who had guarded it to her utmost went with it, but no longer Widow Molly.

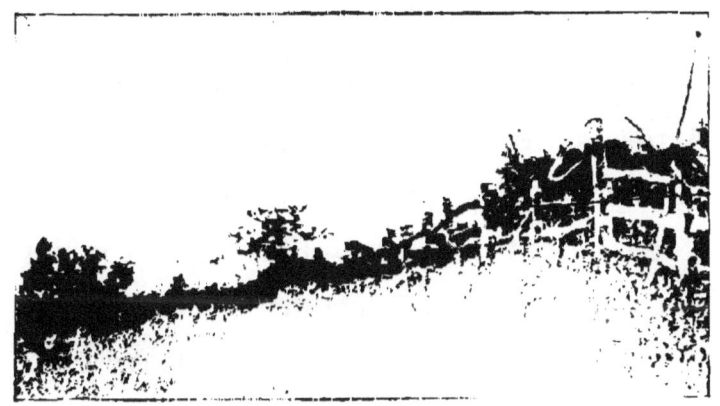

# THE MINERAL-ROD

JOHN was a hand in the paper-mill at
Islip in the twenties.  The old mill is still
standing in the western part of the village,
near the road.  One might almost touch
it with the whip when driving by.  It
represents something of the Islip of the
twenties which was far different from the
Islip of to-day—a quiet, steady-going village, with no incoming of summer residents, and no flutter of gay summer life.
A few sportsmen made their way thither
in the season, but it was a hard day's
stage ride from South Ferry and too far
away to attract even one or two of the
many who were accustomed to leave New
York during the summer.  It was a quiet,
steady-going place, and John was a quiet,
steady-going hand, working in the mill

every day. He had worked there several
years with apparently no thought of doing
anything else. He liked the place. The
merry rumble, the cool moist air always
prevalent, the stream always rushing underneath turning the wheels, and ever slipping
on down the creek and spreading out into
the broad bay. And the tons and tons of
paper that were made and kept going off
somewhere John took great pride in.

But one morning John went to his work
in the mill with his mind no little disturbed.
Nothing had happened out of the ordinary.
His folks were all well and had gone
about their work that morning in the usual
way, with no apprehension of the idea
absorbing his thought. He alone was disturbed. It was plain to see at the mill
that his mind was preoccupied. He talked
little. He did not so much as whistle once
in going up and down stairs about his
work that day. In the night he had had
a singular dream, and he thought it over
and over all day. When he left the mill at

sundown, he had determined that if he should dream the same thing again he would prove the dream.

Several days passed and the impression on his mind had somehow lost its force.

But just a week later to the night, he dreamed again very vividly that at the Point of Woods there was treasure buried between the west end of the woods and the hills which flank the ocean.

The next day he narrated all the particulars of his dream to an intimate friend, Peter by name; and telling him further that as this was the second time he had dreamed the same thing he purposed to get a mineral-rod, go on the Beach, and search over that spot of ground.

Pete's imagination became inflamed also, and he agreed to go with him.

But where was a mineral-rod to be got, or who knew how the magical thing was to be made? If one had a mineral-rod, it was an easy matter to hold it with both hands and walk over ground in which gold or silver was buried. When one came with it near a place where precious metal was hidden, tradition had always asserted that the rod would bend and twist in one's hands and point toward the place of concealment; and such was the mystic attraction between any mass of gold or silver coin and the rod, that no matter how firmly held it would bend down straight when directly over any spot where money was buried.

John knew further from common tradition that this rod was always a crotch cut from a witchhazel bush. But just what additions or modifications were connected with it he had never heard.

He sought out, therefore, the oldest men and talked with them about buried treasure and mineral-rods, and in this way came upon more minute information. He followed up every clew, and at last heard of an old crone living in the middle of the Island who knew how mineral-rods were made, and who in her younger days had used one—proving its power, by holding one in her hands and traversing the garden to find some silver coins which had been concealed there as a test, detecting them at last hid in a cabbage-head.

John went to see her, reaching her cot at dusk and coming home in the evening. To do this he walked sixteen miles.

At first she was reticent.

"It ain't no use to talk of mineral-rods with no gold nor silver to look at nor to feel of."

There was no other way. So John put all the coins he had into her hand, and then she revealed her secret to him. Not only this, but she encouraged him when he told her of his plans. She related what she had done in her younger days when she lived in other parts. And more, she exacted a promise from him of some share of what he would surely find on the Beach.

"It had always been said," she remarked as he was leaving, "and I've heerd it time an' time agin, thet Kidd buried money on thet Beach as well as on Gard'ner's Islan'. Nobody hed found any as yet, because nobody hed s'arched in the right spot. It hed come down from gineration to gineration thet he was along the South Beach many times, an' thet he come in the inlets an' got supplies of the Injins; an' where could he bury treasure thet would be safer than on thet Beach? an' if I was a younger woman, or even now at my age if I hed less rheumatiz, I'd go on to thet Beach an' live there, an' I'd s'arch it fur miles with a min'ral rod."

In his lonely walk home he repeated the directions she had given him to fix them in his mind, for the old crone had been garrulous and had wandered from the particular subject again and again.

" Find a large witchhazel growing in moist, springy ground—near a stream was best. Cut a branch shaped like the letter Y, with prongs rather larger round than a man's thumb, and leave the bark on. In the prong running down from the fork and near the end remove the bark and gouge out a hole large enough to hold a good-sized goosequill, which must be got from a pure white goose. Fill this quill with quicksilver and cover it tightly with kid. Then put this into the hole in the end of the witchhazel crotch, pack a little cotton around it, and replace the bark.

"He must carry a lucky bone in his pocket the while, and carry it with him for days before using the mineral-rod, as well as while using it. All must be done secretly, and no other person should see any part of the process. The rod must be concealed, and it was best to wrap it in an old coat till the spot of search was reached. When going to dig for treasure he must take nothing that had been used—always a new spade or shovel."

John repeated these directions over and over in his walk through the great woods which are gone now almost completely.

The bay and the ocean to the south, the heavy forests north of the line of hamlets along the shores of the bay—such were the conditions at that time. To-day one can picture and realize those conditions to some degree,

"Among the groves at Mastic."

The heavy forest engendered one sense of mystery, the sea engendered another. It is, then, no matter of surprise that in those days superstition and imagination had their rude votaries, and that there were more of this class than we are willing in these years to admit.

It was a month before the mineral-rod was completed, and then a fortnight more went by before all other arrangements and provisions for the expedition were made ready.

At last John and his friend Pete, who believed as confidently as he in buried treasure and the magical power of the mineral-rod to reveal the spot, sailed out of Doxsee's creek and headed their craft for the Point of Woods.

It was a long sail, as they had to beat

all the way across. When they reached the beach, they drew their boat up close to shore and made everything as secure as could be. They had plenty of time, for the daylight still lingered. And as they could not begin their search till after it was fully dark, they concluded to go to the tract of beach, look it thoroughly over, and determine where they would begin the search, and what should be the plan of walking over it with the mineral-rod.

This plan they discussed at great length.

"It's my opinion," said Pete," that the only good way to do is to select some place as a centre, and then walk around this making your circle bigger all the time."

But John opposed this strongly saying, "I don't believe the mineral rod'll work as well that way; and what is more, you're likely to miss going over a good deal of ground, for it's a pretty hard thing to keep the right curve when you're several rods out from the centre."

"But can't you make the circles smaller

and close together," replied Pete, " and then some of the ground 'll be searched over twice ?"

" No," answered John; " there's too much hit-and-miss about that. The best way, and the only right way is to begin on the top of the ridge of them surf hills and walk length-wise of the Beach, just as near a bee-line as possible; and when you've gone over one length of the ground, then turn and walk back within two feet of the first line, and so on till you've gone over the hull ground to the edge of the woods."

Each one held firmly to his own opinion, but John had the advantage in that he had proposed this quest and had made the greater part of the preparations for it.

Darkness had now fully settled. The wind blew out of the east, clear, dry, and cool. The stars shone with the lustre of a cold sky. Large and small, each glistened distinctly in the great dome. The night was beautiful, yet neither of these men

appreciated the beauty or the mystery
that surrounded them.

Unable to agree, they had returned to
their boat.   John took out the mineral-
rod wrapped in an old coat, and Pete took
the two new shovels and threw them over
his shoulder.   John led the way, and they
walked over to the top of the hills.

"Accordin' to my dream," spoke John,
"this is far enough west to begin.   Stick
one shovel down here, and the other we
'll use at the east end in the same way so
as to keep track of what we've been over.
We'll have to change the shovel at each
end every time till we get over to the edge
of the woods."

Pete pushed the shovel into the sand,
and John undid the coat and took out
the mineral-rod.   He was excited as he
grasped each branch, pushed out his arms,
and held the rod in proper position.   His
hands trembled as he started, and the
tighter he grasped the rod—one of the
conditions necessary for him to observe—

the more his hands shook. He walked carefully over the uneven surface of the ridge till he reached the eastern limit according to his dream. Pete drove the shovel into the sand at this end, and they began the search back. Slowly back and forth they walked these long bouts, working laboriously down the slope of the hills. It was tiring work. John's attention was strained again and again. Time after time he would stop, retrace his steps and walk a second time over some spot, going very slowly indeed and clutching the mineral-rod so tightly that the tremor of his hands deceived and balked him. Often he would become so perplexed that he would put the rod into Pete's hands, send him back to the starting-point, and then walk behind him till the uncertain spot had been passed and Pete had said he could feel no bending down or pointing of the rod. The more, however, Pete was called upon to use the rod, the more uncertain he himself grew. Sometimes they both fell to doubting, and then it took them more than an hour to traverse one length of beach and back. To add to their excitement, they were approaching the middle part of the Beach, the very place where they believed they would surely find an indication of buried gold.

The night, however, had gone faster than they were aware. The day was breaking faintly in the east, and when searching up to the top of a small hillock, they suddenly noticed the dawn.

The search they both knew must be conducted at night.

What was it best to do?

"We've got to stop, make marks of some kind to show us where we left off, and come back again at dark to-night and go over the rest of the ground."

So they wrapped the mineral-rod up in the coat, heaped up a little mound of sand where both shovels stood, took these, and made their way to the boat.

They were hungry, but they did not

delay to eat. It was best for them, they felt, to get away from that part of the Beach.

Accordingly they got their boat under way, and as they sailed eastward along the Beach, tired and chilly, they ate their breakfast. After they had sailed four or five miles they headed out into the bay. When the sun was well up, they put about and steered directly for the Beach. On the flats they anchored, lay down in their boat, and went to sleep.

Just before dusk that night they were back at the Point of Woods. As soon as the day had completely gone they stood up the shovels in the mounds they had made at daybreak that morning, undid again the mineral-rod and began anew the search. They worked carefully for three hours, becoming at times confused, as on the previous night, and frequently retracing their steps and going over many places a second time. They had worked their way, however, nearly over to the outskirts of the wood. John had come to a small hillock, perhaps four feet high, and was walking up over it when suddenly he felt the end of the rod drawn strongly down. He could not mistake this. Some decided force had pulled the end of the mineral-rod down, and it pointed obliquely to the hillock.

"There's no doubt this time," he said as he stepped back a few paces, feeling as he did so some decrease in the force exerted upon the end of the mineral-rod. "You get the shovel to the west and bring the old coat here. I'll get the shovel behind us. This, I tell you, is the very spot."

Each of them was highly excited as he came back to the hillock.

"Hold on," said John as he restrained Pete from striking his shovel into the sand. "Let's begin together, and remember that come whatever will, not one word must be spoken while we're digging—not a sound till we've got what there is here completely out of the hole."

"Now I'm ready," said John after a second, and they began to dig vigorously.

It proved warm work, and shortly each in silence took off his coat and laid it with the mineral-rod. Half an hour passed and there was a decided slackening in the rate of digging. Whether they were beginning to doubt or not, nothing could be said. At length Pete's shovel struck something. He drove it into the same spot for another shovelful. As it struck he heard a hollow thud. Then John struck it with his shovel and again came the same hollow sound.

There was something here surely, each thought, yet neither of them spoke. They were unable to make out exactly what it was, other than wood of some sort, for their shovels cut into it as they struck it. But every time there came the hollow sound.

John began to widen the hole they were digging, and Pete soon noticed this, and followed John's example.

The wind now blew a strong breeze, for

it had gradually risen as the night had progressed.

Threatening clouds were bunching up and drifting across the sky. All the signs indicated a coming southeasterly storm, and it would likely be severe while it lasted.

Both men thought of this, for they were weatherwise. Still they might dig on two hours longer if necessary.

After widening the hole, they dug toward the centre, where they had struck the wood, and then down by the mysterious dark object. The sky was becoming more obscured and they could not see so well, even though the pupils of their eyes were dilated to the utmost. They dug farther down beside it. John reached a place where he got his shovel underside and began to pry. Something gave way slightly. He dug again, and got his shovel farther under and pried harder. The dark object began to crack. Pete seized hold of it with both hands and exerted all his strength. It gave way and they rolled it out of the hole. Then they examined it with their hands, feeling it all over. It was the hollow stump of a tree. John ran his arm to the bottom of the hole several times, but took out nothing but sand.

He stood a moment contemplating and then with his foot he pushed it angrily back into the hole. Quickly he turned, gathered up the coats and his shovel, and set off for the boat. Pete followed, and not a word was uttered.

They got their boat under way, each maintaining silence. The wind was free. John let the sheet run, and they swept out into the broad bay. The waves ran high. Their boat, as if a thing of life and spirit, would poise on the top of a wave while its crest broke with a rushing sound, and then drop gradually behind into its trough. Then the next wave would come up astern and bear them up in the same manner. And so their little boat rode each wave and swept onward. The rhythmic movement of the boat and waves had a quieting and solacing effect upon these disappointed argonauts. Half-way across, Pete spoke and said, " John, that hillock was covered with brier-bushes, you remember. That must have been a brier that pulled down the end of the rod."

John made no reply to this, but ten minutes later he broke his silence :

" Pete," he said suddenly, "hand me that stone forward with the rope tied to it. Now give me that old coat. No, hold on! You come here and steer."

He moved forward, then tied the stone tightly to the old coat. Standing up, he threw the bundle from him with all his might, saying as he did so, " There goes that cussed thing overboard. I wish to thunder I had the money I put into that darned old granny's hands six weeks ago."

Having proved his dream, John returned to his work in the mill. He worked there contentedly several years longer. He liked the place. The merry rumble, the stream always rushing underneath, turning the wheels and slipping on down the creek and spreading out into the broad bay. And the tons and tons of paper that were made and kept going off somewhere John took greater pride in than ever.

# NOTES.

PAGE 22.

Watch Hill is a prominent hill on the Beach opposite Patchogue.

PAGE 41.

Quanch is a landing-place on the Beach opposite Otis's Point.

PAGE 46.

Between the years 1710 and 1720 as many as twenty whales were taken in a single season by the crews on the Beach.

PAGE 47.

Fiddleton is a mile and a half west of Quanch.

Pickety Rough is a strip of beach east of Point o' Woods, so called because of the prickly growth of bushes there.

PAGE 59.

" The Gore in the Hills " was a name given to a tract of land near Yaphank, over which a dispute arose in the last century. This dispute was settled by arbitration in 1753.

## PAGE 60.

" Squasux "—the Indian name for the landing on Carman's River, at the end of the Brookhaven Neck road.

The last owner of the house here alluded to was the late Joseph Carman.

## PAGE 62.

" The Inlet " referred to began to close up in the early part of this century. Small coasting vessels sailed out of this inlet as late as 1816. The inlet kept filling in, however, and the small channel was at last blocked by a brig which went ashore at the mouth of it. Soon after the channel filled up com pletely. This brig was loaded with grindstones, and on this account was popularly called the "Grind-stone Brig." This spot of beach has been known ever since as "Old Inlet." It is opposite the extreme eastern end of Bellport.

## PAGES 63 and 64.

This incident actually occurred as here related.

## PAGE 65.

Between the years 1780 and 1785 the persecution of Judge William Smith by certain townspeople was so great that he was compelled, in order to save his life, to give up a part of his estate to them.

His barns were burned to the ground, with a loss of thirty horses, and all his orchards were girdled. The burning of his dwelling was intended, but for some cause this intention was not carried out.

He had, moreover, a narrow escape from being

shot through his bedroom window as he was going
to bed. It so happened that his wife was all the
time between him and the window, and the three
men outside could not cover him with their muskets
without covering her at the same time.

Judge William Smith lived at the Manor of St.
George (Smith's Point) where the late Egbert Tan-
gier Smith resided nearly the whole of his life.

## PAGE 99.

The landing, now a thing of the past, was on the
shore now embraced in Wood Acres—the estate of
Mr. George T. Lyman at Bellport.

## PAGE 124.

Clam Hollow is situated midway between Bellport and Brookhaven. Within the past forty years
the heavy woods have been cut down, the road
made somewhat straighter, the hollow raised several
feet, and the western hill cut down.

Brewster's Brook, previously called Dayton's
Brook, but known for the past sixty years as Os-
born's Brook, is in the eastern part of Bellport at
the foot of the hill.

## PAGE 128.

The Mills was the old name for South Haven
because of the grist and saw mills situated there at
the foot of the pond.

## PAGE 137.

"Near Southampton," etc., about a mile west of
"St. Andrews by the Sea."

## PAGE 139.

After the breaking up of the ship, it was the custom of certain farmers in the fall, when the neap tides would permit, to plow along the shore, and the waves cutting over the upturned furrows would wash out these Spanish coins.

## PAGE 143.

The present residence alluded to was known for a long time as the Corse Place.

Champlin's stood where the South Side Club House now stands.

## PAGE 149.

" Inlet near the Manor of St. George."    See note to page 62.

## PAGE 171.

" Penataquit "—an Indian word—the early post-office name of Bay Shore.

## PAGE 173.

Long Cove is about three-quarters of a mile east of Watch Hill.